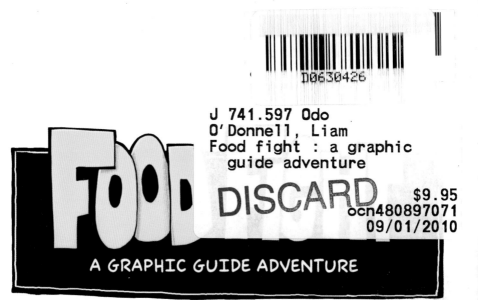

FOOD FIGHT

A GRAPHIC GUIDE ADVENTURE

WRITTEN BY	ILLUSTRATED BY
LIAM O'DONNELL	**MIKE DEAS**

ORCA BOOK PUBLISHERS

For Mom. —LOD

Thanks to Nancy for her continued support. —MD

Library and Archives Canada Cataloguing in Publication

O'Donnell, Liam, 1970-

Food fight : a graphic guide adventure / written by Liam O'Donnell ;
illustrated by Mike Deas.

ISBN 978-1-55469-067-1

I. Deas, Mike, 1982- II. Title.

PS8579.D647F66 2010   j741.5'971   C2009-906857-5

First published in the United States, 2010
Library of Congress Control Number: 2009940900

Summary: Devin and Nadia are in a desperate race to stop a multinational corporation
from gaining control of the food supply and ruining their mother's career.

Orca Book Publishers gratefully acknowledges the support for its publishing programs provided
by the following agencies: the Government of Canada through the Canada Book Fund and the
Canada Council for the Arts, and the Province of British Columbia through the BC Arts Council
and the Book Publishing Tax Credit.

Cover and interior artwork by Mike Deas
Cover layout by Teresa Bubela
Author photo by Melanie McBride • Illustrator photo by Ellen Ho

ORCA BOOK PUBLISHERS	ORCA BOOK PUBLISHERS
PO Box 5626, STN. B	PO Box 468
VICTORIA, BC CANADA	CUSTER, WA USA
V8R 6S4	98240-0468

www.orcabook.com
Printed and bound in Hong Kong.
13 12 11 10 • 4 3 2 1

CHAPTER 1
DIG IT

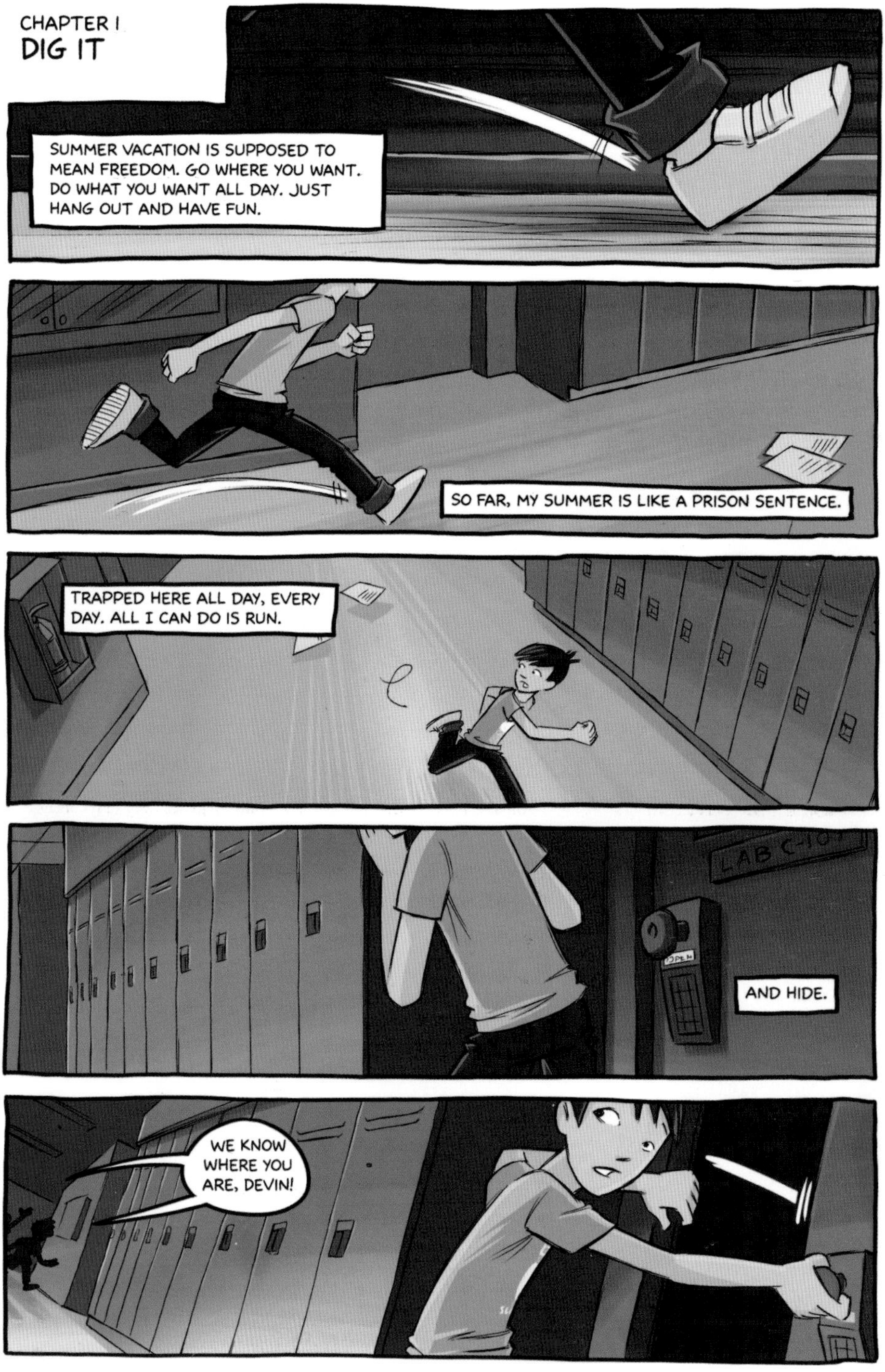
SUMMER VACATION IS SUPPOSED TO MEAN FREEDOM. GO WHERE YOU WANT. DO WHAT YOU WANT ALL DAY. JUST HANG OUT AND HAVE FUN.
SO FAR, MY SUMMER IS LIKE A PRISON SENTENCE.
TRAPPED HERE ALL DAY, EVERY DAY. ALL I CAN DO IS RUN.
AND HIDE.
WE KNOW WHERE YOU ARE, DEVIN!

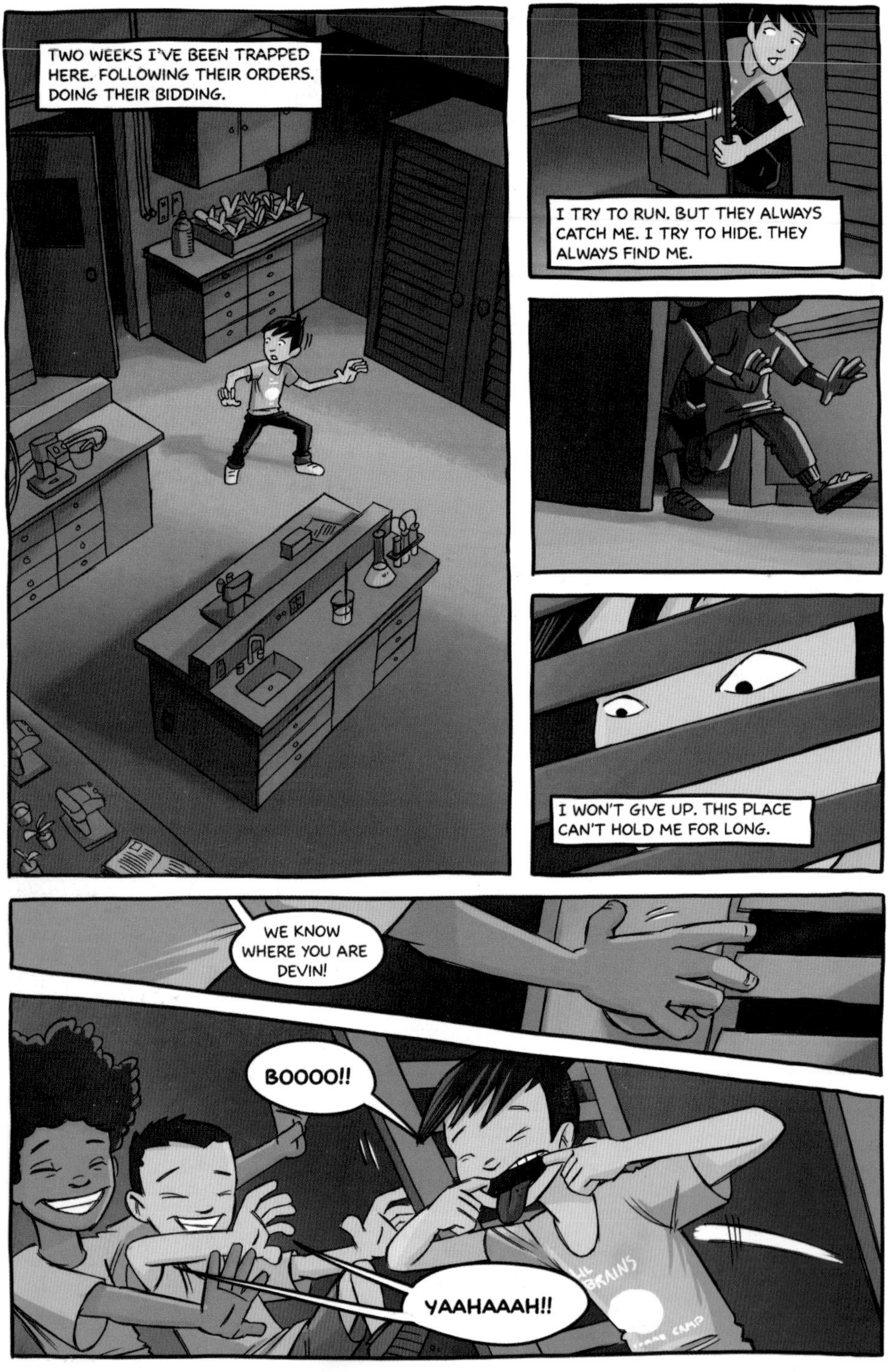
TWO WEEKS I'VE BEEN TRAPPED HERE. FOLLOWING THEIR ORDERS. DOING THEIR BIDDING.
I TRY TO RUN. BUT THEY ALWAYS CATCH ME. I TRY TO HIDE. THEY ALWAYS FIND ME.
I WON'T GIVE UP. THIS PLACE CAN'T HOLD ME FOR LONG.
WE KNOW WHERE YOU ARE DEVIN!
BOOOO!!
YAAHAAAH!!

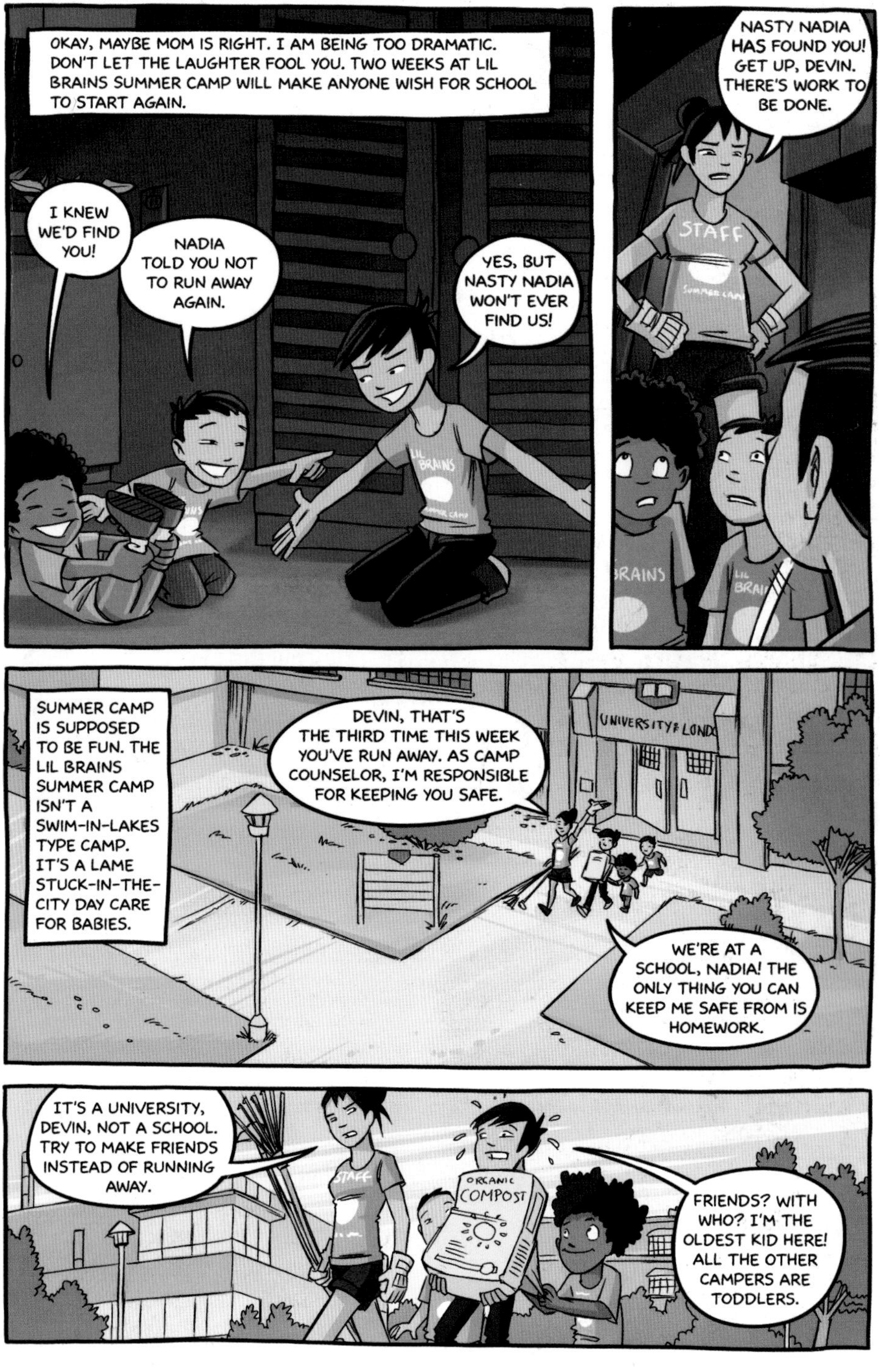
OKAY, MAYBE MOM IS RIGHT. I AM BEING TOO DRAMATIC. DON'T LET THE LAUGHTER FOOL YOU. TWO WEEKS AT LIL BRAINS SUMMER CAMP WILL MAKE ANYONE WISH FOR SCHOOL TO START AGAIN.
I KNEW WE'D FIND YOU!
NADIA TOLD YOU NOT TO RUN AWAY AGAIN.
YES, BUT NASTY NADIA WON'T EVER FIND US!
NASTY NADIA HAS FOUND YOU! GET UP, DEVIN. THERE'S WORK TO BE DONE.
STAFF
SUMMER CAMP IS SUPPOSED TO BE FUN. THE LIL BRAINS SUMMER CAMP ISN'T A SWIM-IN-LAKES TYPE CAMP. IT'S A LAME STUCK-IN-THE-CITY DAY CARE FOR BABIES.
DEVIN, THAT'S THE THIRD TIME THIS WEEK YOU'VE RUN AWAY. AS CAMP COUNSELOR, I'M RESPONSIBLE FOR KEEPING YOU SAFE.
WE'RE AT A SCHOOL, NADIA! THE ONLY THING YOU CAN KEEP ME SAFE FROM IS HOMEWORK.
IT'S A UNIVERSITY, DEVIN, NOT A SCHOOL. TRY TO MAKE FRIENDS INSTEAD OF RUNNING AWAY.
ORGANIC COMPOST
FRIENDS? WITH WHO? I'M THE OLDEST KID HERE! ALL THE OTHER CAMPERS ARE TODDLERS.

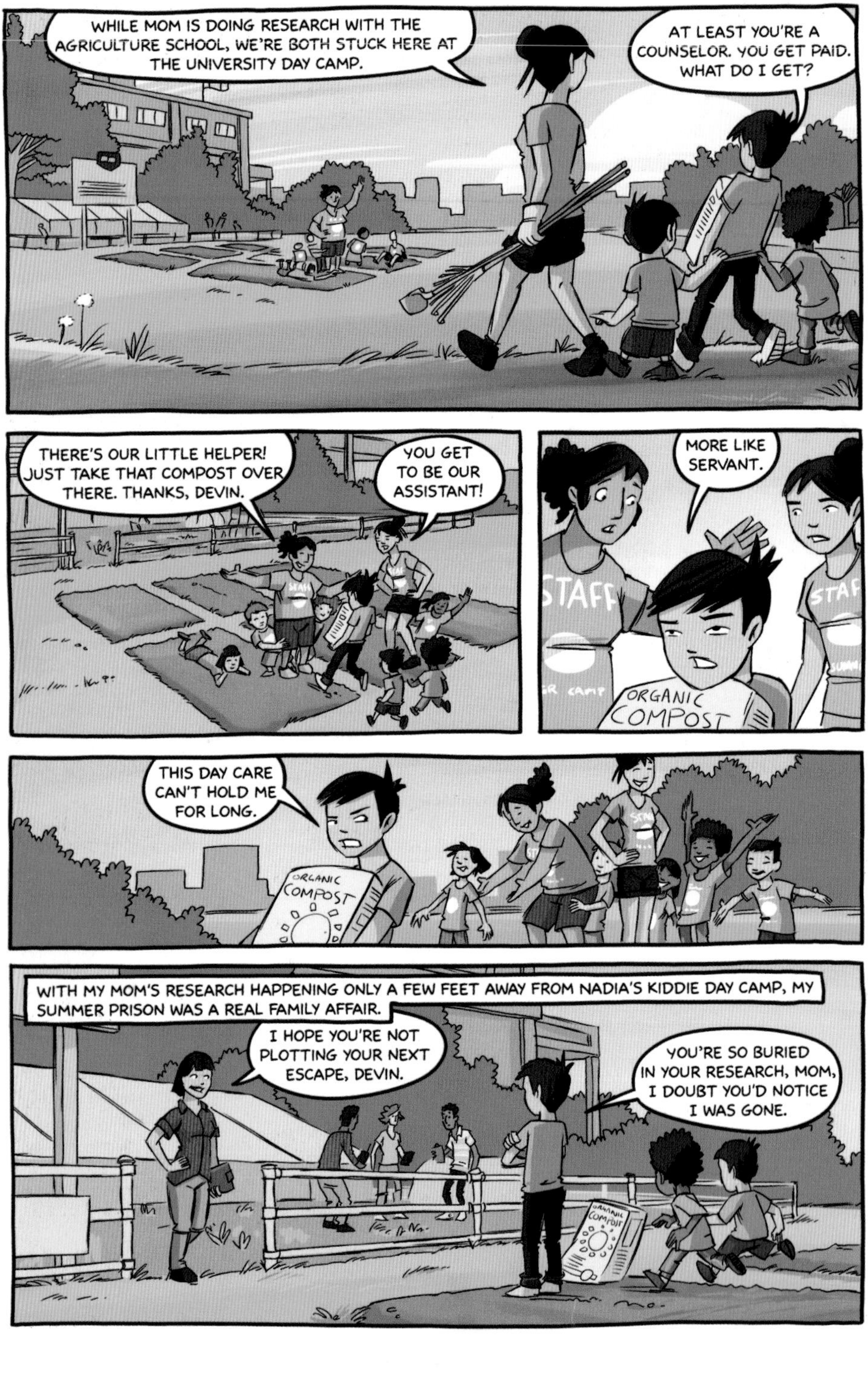
WHILE MOM IS DOING RESEARCH WITH THE AGRICULTURE SCHOOL, WE'RE BOTH STUCK HERE AT THE UNIVERSITY DAY CAMP.
AT LEAST YOU'RE A COUNSELOR. YOU GET PAID. WHAT DO I GET?
THERE'S OUR LITTLE HELPER! JUST TAKE THAT COMPOST OVER THERE. THANKS, DEVIN.
YOU GET TO BE OUR ASSISTANT!
MORE LIKE SERVANT.
STAFF
ORGANIC COMPOST
THIS DAY CARE CAN'T HOLD ME FOR LONG.
ORGANIC COMPOST
WITH MY MOM'S RESEARCH HAPPENING ONLY A FEW FEET AWAY FROM NADIA'S KIDDIE DAY CAMP, MY SUMMER PRISON WAS A REAL FAMILY AFFAIR.
I HOPE YOU'RE NOT PLOTTING YOUR NEXT ESCAPE, DEVIN.
YOU'RE SO BURIED IN YOUR RESEARCH, MOM, I DOUBT YOU'D NOTICE I WAS GONE.

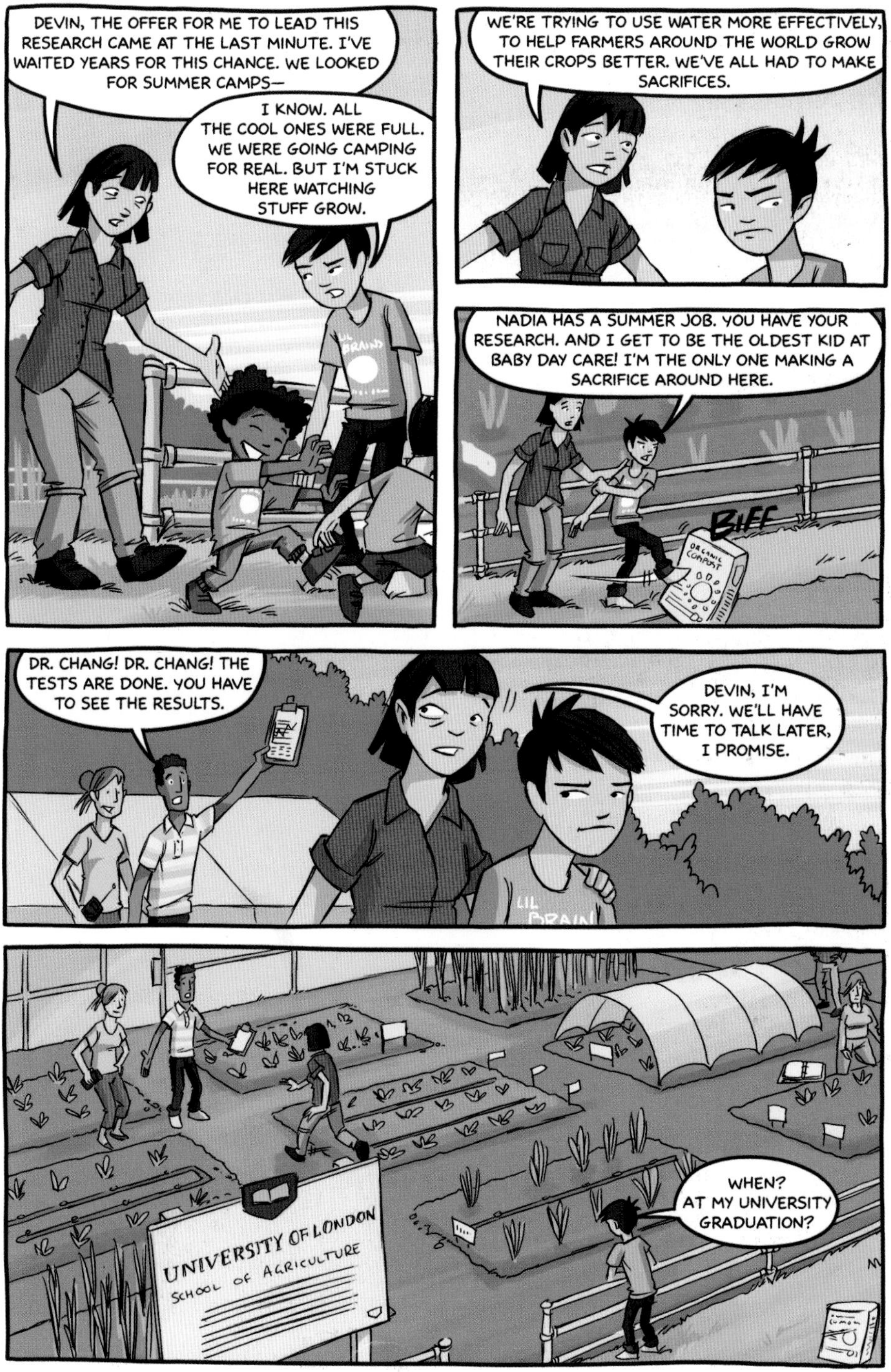
DEVIN, THE OFFER FOR ME TO LEAD THIS RESEARCH CAME AT THE LAST MINUTE. I'VE WAITED YEARS FOR THIS CHANCE. WE LOOKED FOR SUMMER CAMPS—
I KNOW. ALL THE COOL ONES WERE FULL. WE WERE GOING CAMPING FOR REAL. BUT I'M STUCK HERE WATCHING STUFF GROW.
LIL BRAIN
WE'RE TRYING TO USE WATER MORE EFFECTIVELY, TO HELP FARMERS AROUND THE WORLD GROW THEIR CROPS BETTER. WE'VE ALL HAD TO MAKE SACRIFICES.
NADIA HAS A SUMMER JOB. YOU HAVE YOUR RESEARCH. AND I GET TO BE THE OLDEST KID AT BABY DAY CARE! I'M THE ONLY ONE MAKING A SACRIFICE AROUND HERE.
BIFF
ORGANIC COMPOST
DR. CHANG! DR. CHANG! THE TESTS ARE DONE. YOU HAVE TO SEE THE RESULTS.
DEVIN, I'M SORRY. WE'LL HAVE TIME TO TALK LATER, I PROMISE.
LIL BRAIN
UNIVERSITY OF LONDON
SCHOOL OF AGRICULTURE
WHEN? AT MY UNIVERSITY GRADUATION?

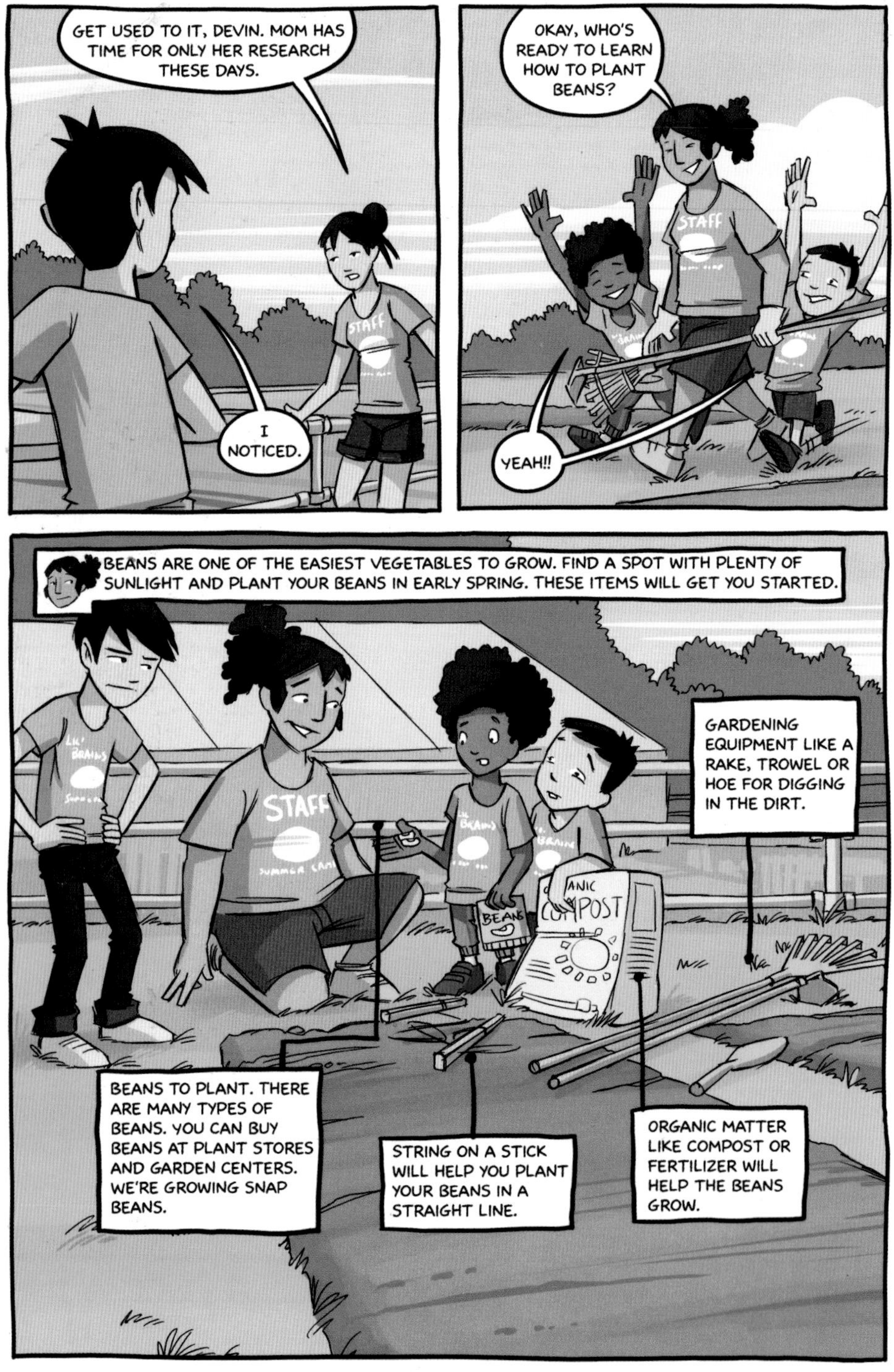
GET USED TO IT, DEVIN. MOM HAS TIME FOR ONLY HER RESEARCH THESE DAYS.
I NOTICED.
OKAY, WHO'S READY TO LEARN HOW TO PLANT BEANS?
YEAH!!
BEANS ARE ONE OF THE EASIEST VEGETABLES TO GROW. FIND A SPOT WITH PLENTY OF SUNLIGHT AND PLANT YOUR BEANS IN EARLY SPRING. THESE ITEMS WILL GET YOU STARTED.
GARDENING EQUIPMENT LIKE A RAKE, TROWEL OR HOE FOR DIGGING IN THE DIRT.
BEANS TO PLANT. THERE ARE MANY TYPES OF BEANS. YOU CAN BUY BEANS AT PLANT STORES AND GARDEN CENTERS. WE'RE GROWING SNAP BEANS.
STRING ON A STICK WILL HELP YOU PLANT YOUR BEANS IN A STRAIGHT LINE.
ORGANIC MATTER LIKE COMPOST OR FERTILIZER WILL HELP THE BEANS GROW.

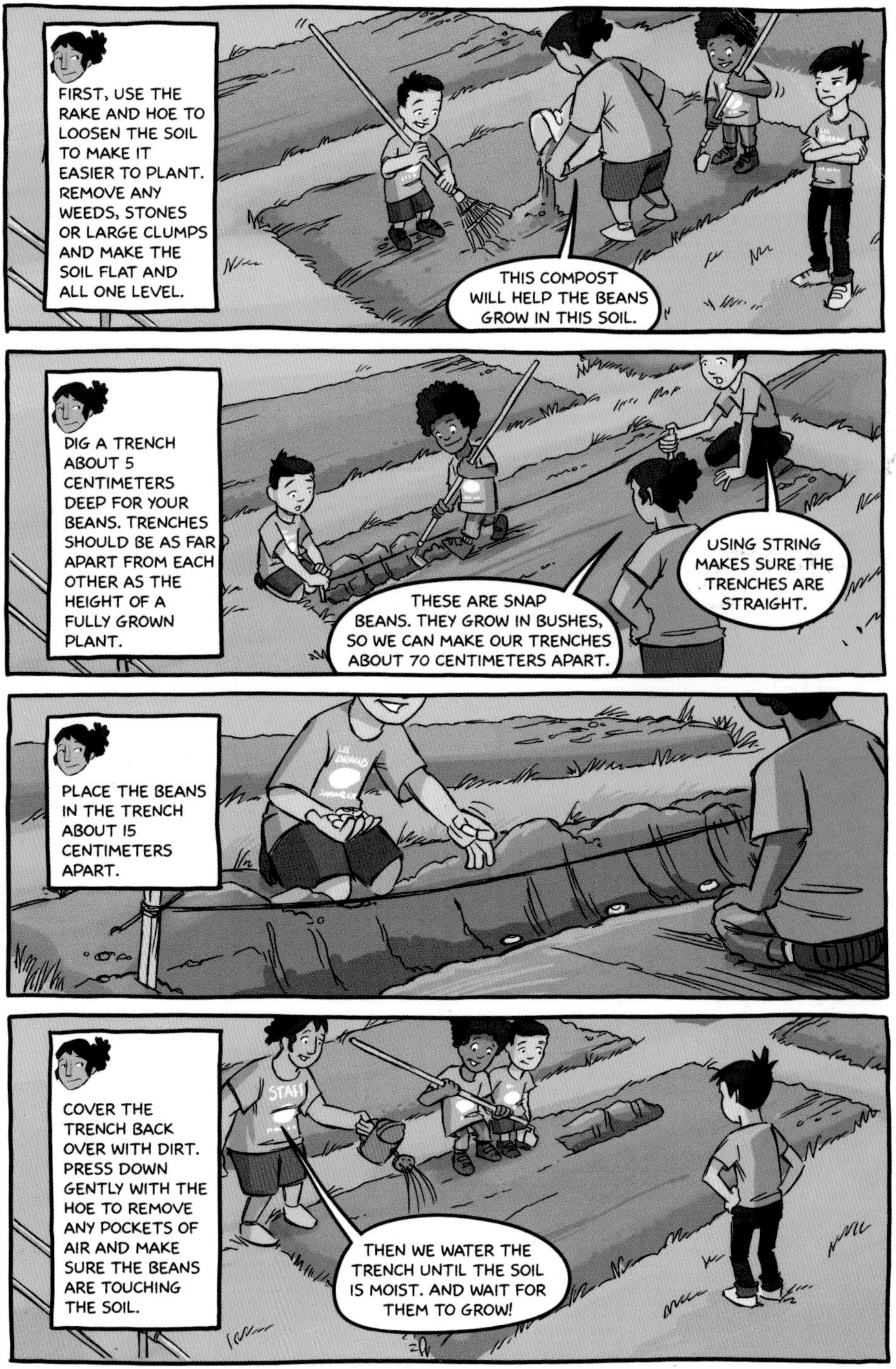
FIRST, USE THE RAKE AND HOE TO LOOSEN THE SOIL TO MAKE IT EASIER TO PLANT. REMOVE ANY WEEDS, STONES OR LARGE CLUMPS AND MAKE THE SOIL FLAT AND ALL ONE LEVEL.
THIS COMPOST WILL HELP THE BEANS GROW IN THIS SOIL.
DIG A TRENCH ABOUT 5 CENTIMETERS DEEP FOR YOUR BEANS. TRENCHES SHOULD BE AS FAR APART FROM EACH OTHER AS THE HEIGHT OF A FULLY GROWN PLANT.
THESE ARE SNAP BEANS. THEY GROW IN BUSHES, SO WE CAN MAKE OUR TRENCHES ABOUT 70 CENTIMETERS APART.
USING STRING MAKES SURE THE TRENCHES ARE STRAIGHT.
PLACE THE BEANS IN THE TRENCH ABOUT 15 CENTIMETERS APART.
COVER THE TRENCH BACK OVER WITH DIRT. PRESS DOWN GENTLY WITH THE HOE TO REMOVE ANY POCKETS OF AIR AND MAKE SURE THE BEANS ARE TOUCHING THE SOIL.
STAFF
THEN WE WATER THE TRENCH UNTIL THE SOIL IS MOIST. AND WAIT FOR THEM TO GROW!

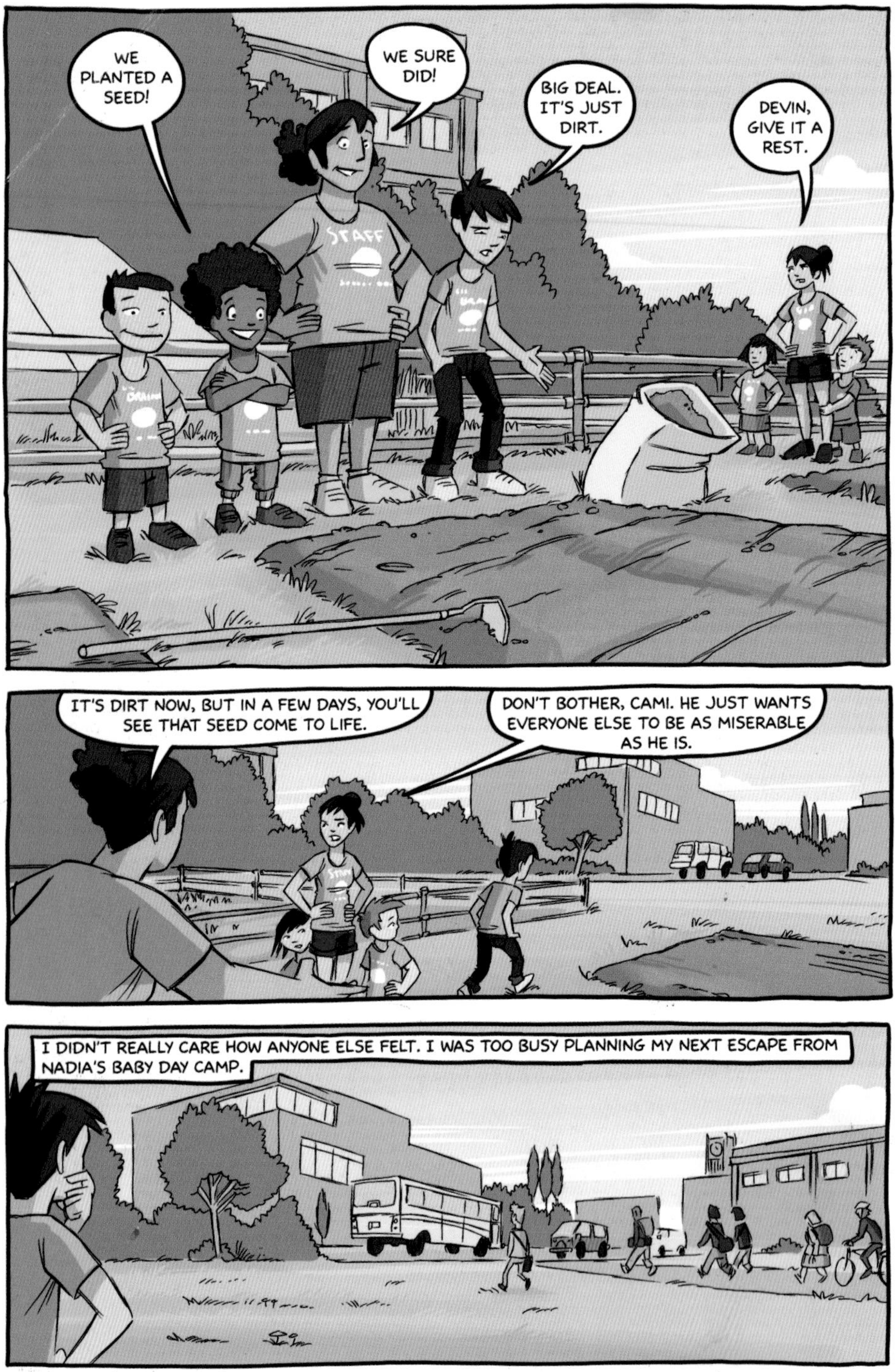
WE PLANTED A SEED!
WE SURE DID!
BIG DEAL. IT'S JUST DIRT.
DEVIN, GIVE IT A REST.
IT'S DIRT NOW, BUT IN A FEW DAYS, YOU'LL SEE THAT SEED COME TO LIFE.
DON'T BOTHER, CAMI. HE JUST WANTS EVERYONE ELSE TO BE AS MISERABLE AS HE IS.
I DIDN'T REALLY CARE HOW ANYONE ELSE FELT. I WAS TOO BUSY PLANNING MY NEXT ESCAPE FROM NADIA'S BABY DAY CAMP.

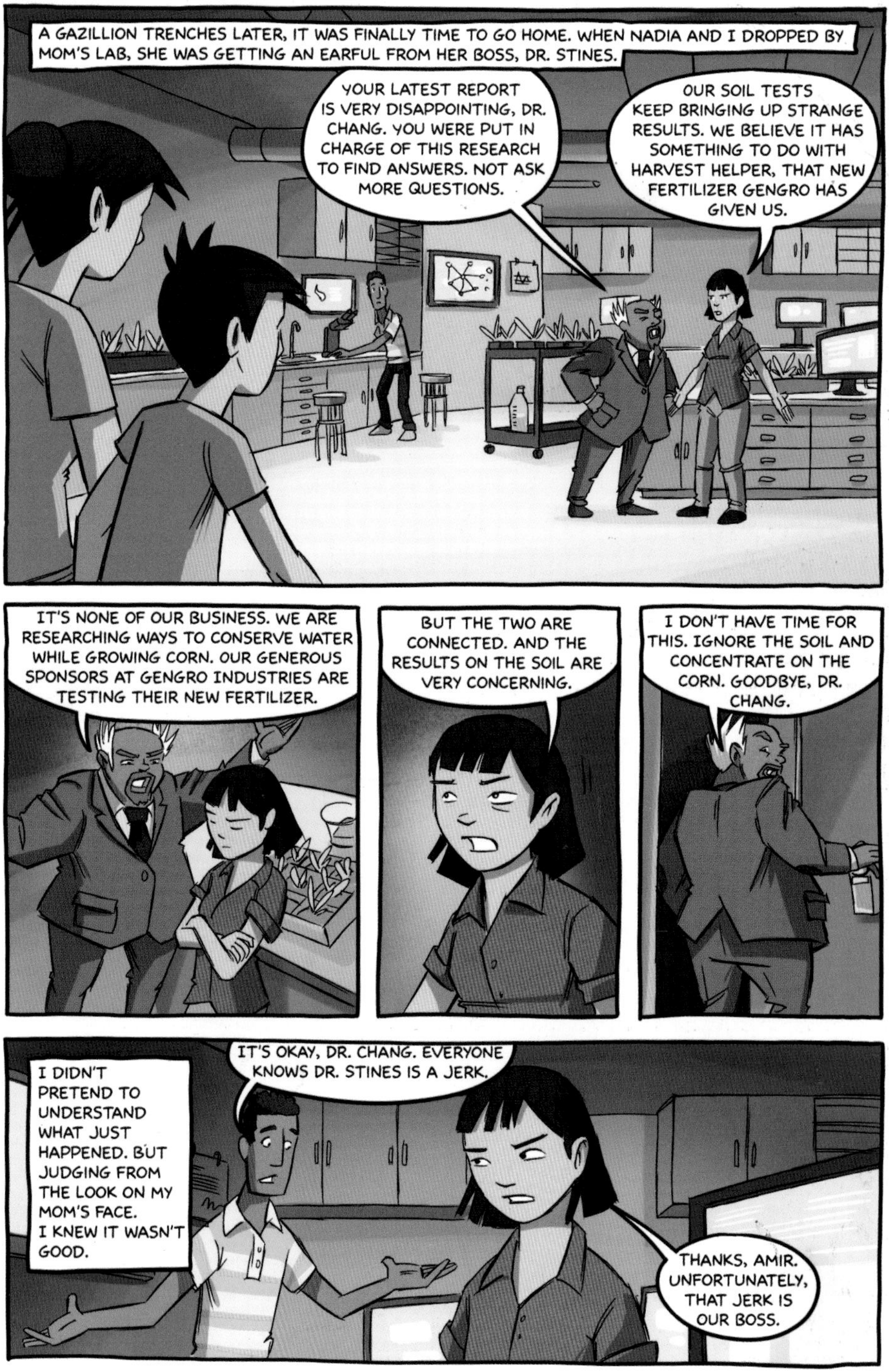
A GAZILLION TRENCHES LATER, IT WAS FINALLY TIME TO GO HOME. WHEN NADIA AND I DROPPED BY MOM'S LAB, SHE WAS GETTING AN EARFUL FROM HER BOSS, DR. STINES.
YOUR LATEST REPORT IS VERY DISAPPOINTING, DR. CHANG. YOU WERE PUT IN CHARGE OF THIS RESEARCH TO FIND ANSWERS. NOT ASK MORE QUESTIONS.
OUR SOIL TESTS KEEP BRINGING UP STRANGE RESULTS. WE BELIEVE IT HAS SOMETHING TO DO WITH HARVEST HELPER, THAT NEW FERTILIZER GENGRO HAS GIVEN US.
IT'S NONE OF OUR BUSINESS. WE ARE RESEARCHING WAYS TO CONSERVE WATER WHILE GROWING CORN. OUR GENEROUS SPONSORS AT GENGRO INDUSTRIES ARE TESTING THEIR NEW FERTILIZER.
BUT THE TWO ARE CONNECTED. AND THE RESULTS ON THE SOIL ARE VERY CONCERNING.
I DON'T HAVE TIME FOR THIS. IGNORE THE SOIL AND CONCENTRATE ON THE CORN. GOODBYE, DR. CHANG.
I DIDN'T PRETEND TO UNDERSTAND WHAT JUST HAPPENED. BUT JUDGING FROM THE LOOK ON MY MOM'S FACE. I KNEW IT WASN'T GOOD.
IT'S OKAY, DR. CHANG. EVERYONE KNOWS DR. STINES IS A JERK.
THANKS, AMIR. UNFORTUNATELY, THAT JERK IS OUR BOSS.

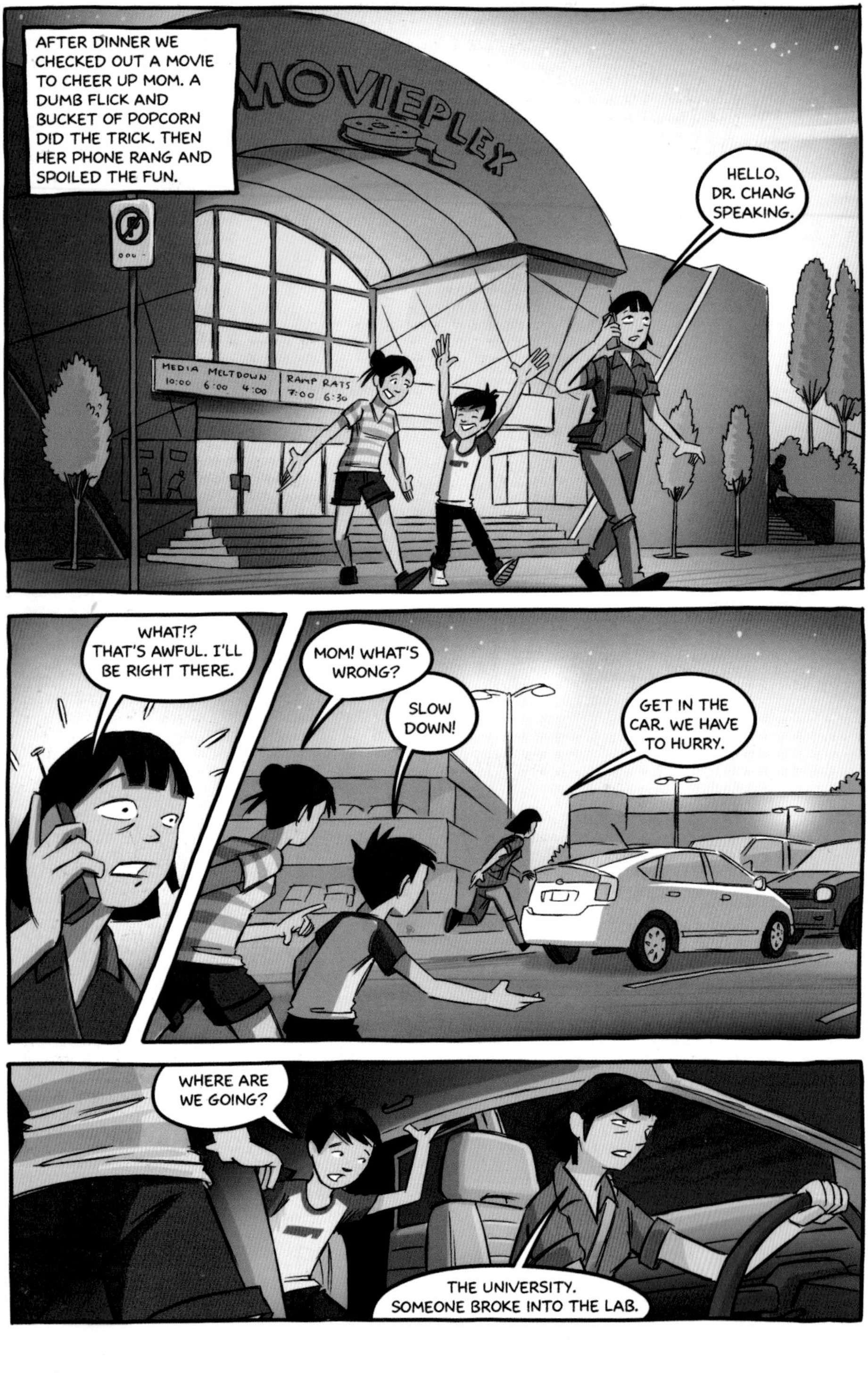
AFTER DINNER WE CHECKED OUT A MOVIE TO CHEER UP MOM. A DUMB FLICK AND BUCKET OF POPCORN DID THE TRICK. THEN HER PHONE RANG AND SPOILED THE FUN.
MOVIEPLEX
MEDIA MELTDOWN 10:00 6:00 4:00
RAMP RATS 7:00 6:30
HELLO, DR. CHANG SPEAKING.
WHAT!? THAT'S AWFUL. I'LL BE RIGHT THERE.
MOM! WHAT'S WRONG?
SLOW DOWN!
GET IN THE CAR. WE HAVE TO HURRY.
WHERE ARE WE GOING?
THE UNIVERSITY. SOMEONE BROKE INTO THE LAB.

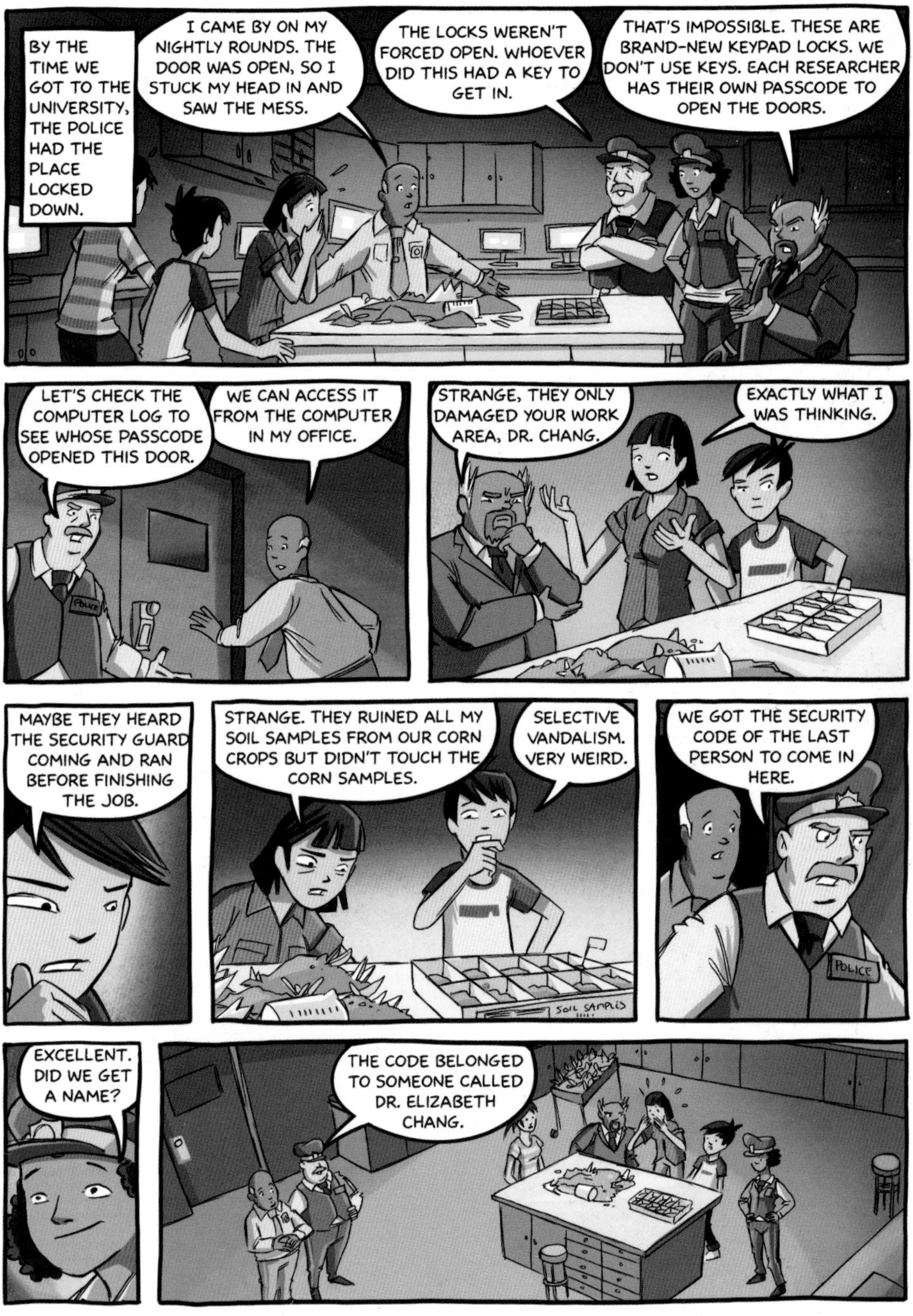
BY THE TIME WE GOT TO THE UNIVERSITY, THE POLICE HAD THE PLACE LOCKED DOWN.
I CAME BY ON MY NIGHTLY ROUNDS. THE DOOR WAS OPEN, SO I STUCK MY HEAD IN AND SAW THE MESS.
THE LOCKS WEREN'T FORCED OPEN. WHOEVER DID THIS HAD A KEY TO GET IN.
THAT'S IMPOSSIBLE. THESE ARE BRAND-NEW KEYPAD LOCKS. WE DON'T USE KEYS. EACH RESEARCHER HAS THEIR OWN PASSCODE TO OPEN THE DOORS.
LET'S CHECK THE COMPUTER LOG TO SEE WHOSE PASSCODE OPENED THIS DOOR.
WE CAN ACCESS IT FROM THE COMPUTER IN MY OFFICE.
POLICE
STRANGE, THEY ONLY DAMAGED YOUR WORK AREA, DR. CHANG.
EXACTLY WHAT I WAS THINKING.
MAYBE THEY HEARD THE SECURITY GUARD COMING AND RAN BEFORE FINISHING THE JOB.
STRANGE. THEY RUINED ALL MY SOIL SAMPLES FROM OUR CORN CROPS BUT DIDN'T TOUCH THE CORN SAMPLES.
SELECTIVE VANDALISM. VERY WEIRD.
SOIL SAMPLES
WE GOT THE SECURITY CODE OF THE LAST PERSON TO COME IN HERE.
POLICE
EXCELLENT. DID WE GET A NAME?
THE CODE BELONGED TO SOMEONE CALLED DR. ELIZABETH CHANG.

CHAPTER 2

GREAT ESCAPE II

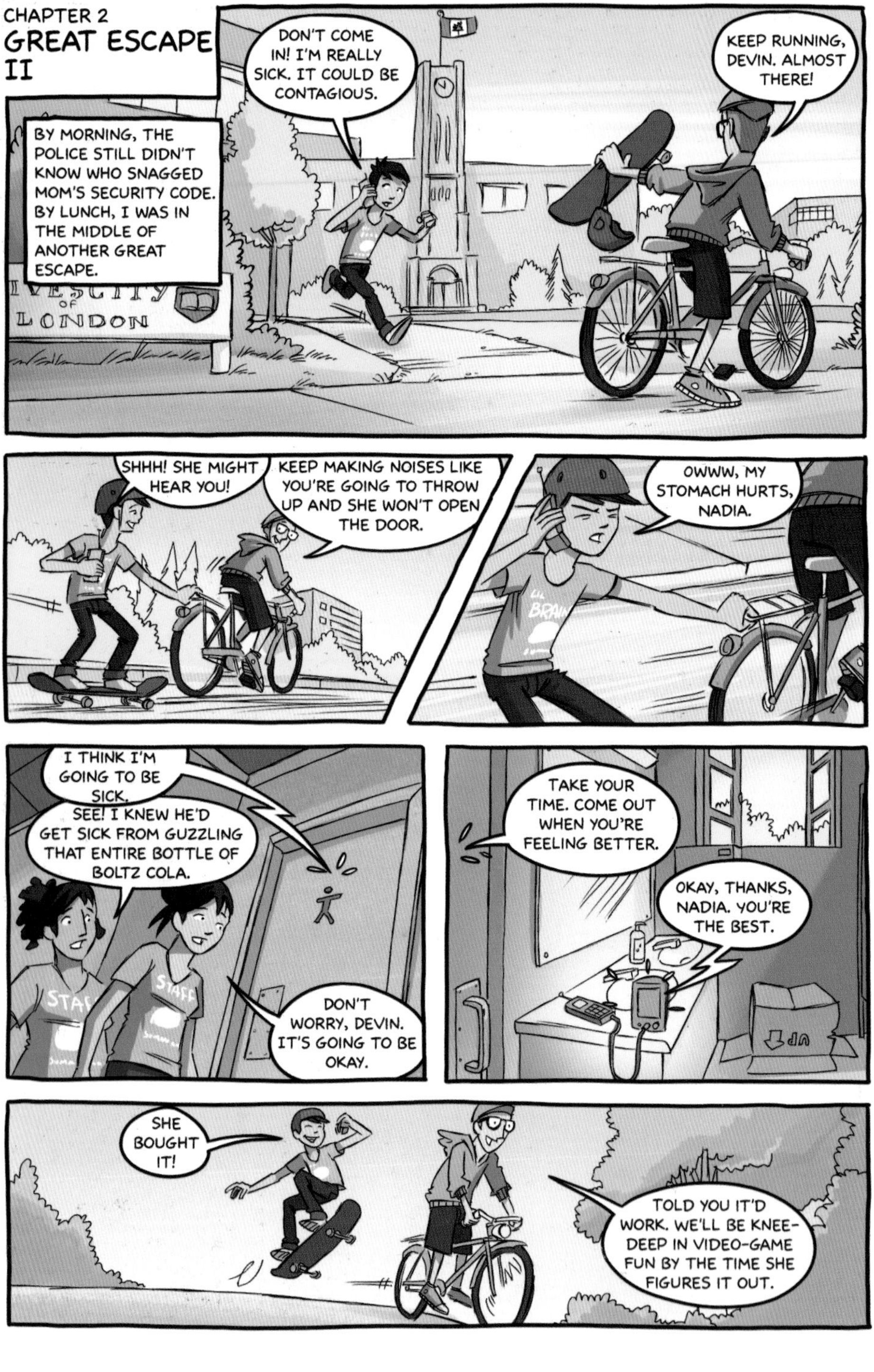
BY MORNING, THE POLICE STILL DIDN'T KNOW WHO SNAGGED MOM'S SECURITY CODE. BY LUNCH, I WAS IN THE MIDDLE OF ANOTHER GREAT ESCAPE.
DON'T COME IN! I'M REALLY SICK. IT COULD BE CONTAGIOUS.
KEEP RUNNING, DEVIN. ALMOST THERE!
LONDON
SHHH! SHE MIGHT HEAR YOU!
KEEP MAKING NOISES LIKE YOU'RE GOING TO THROW UP AND SHE WON'T OPEN THE DOOR.
OWWW, MY STOMACH HURTS, NADIA.
I THINK I'M GOING TO BE SICK.
SEE! I KNEW HE'D GET SICK FROM GUZZLING THAT ENTIRE BOTTLE OF BOLTZ COLA.
STAFF
STAFF
DON'T WORRY, DEVIN. IT'S GOING TO BE OKAY.
TAKE YOUR TIME. COME OUT WHEN YOU'RE FEELING BETTER.
OKAY, THANKS, NADIA. YOU'RE THE BEST.
SHE BOUGHT IT!
TOLD YOU IT'D WORK. WE'LL BE KNEE-DEEP IN VIDEO-GAME FUN BY THE TIME SHE FIGURES IT OUT.

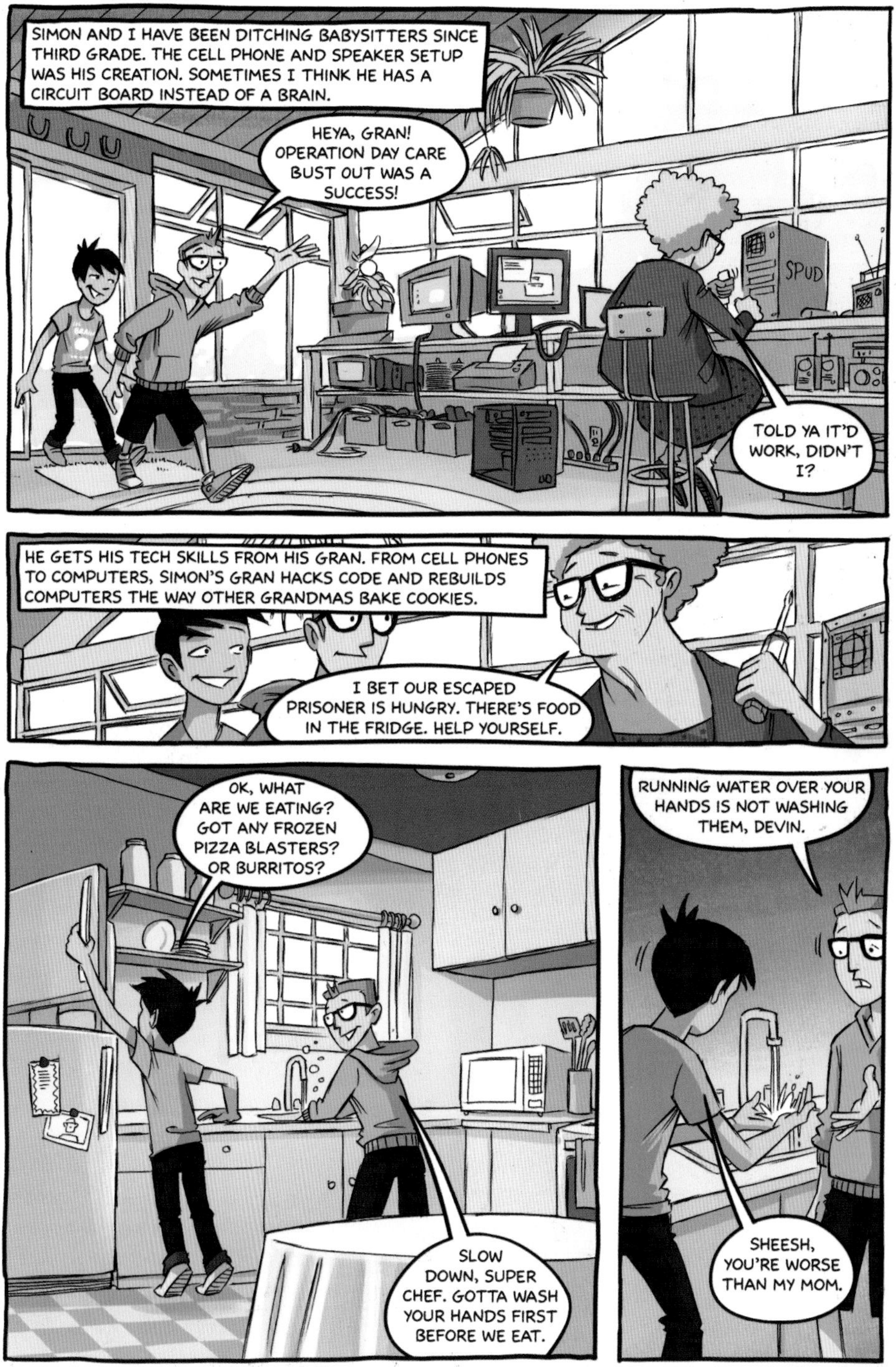
SIMON AND I HAVE BEEN DITCHING BABYSITTERS SINCE THIRD GRADE. THE CELL PHONE AND SPEAKER SETUP WAS HIS CREATION. SOMETIMES I THINK HE HAS A CIRCUIT BOARD INSTEAD OF A BRAIN.
HEYA, GRAN! OPERATION DAY CARE BUST OUT WAS A SUCCESS!
SPUD
TOLD YA IT'D WORK, DIDN'T I?
HE GETS HIS TECH SKILLS FROM HIS GRAN. FROM CELL PHONES TO COMPUTERS, SIMON'S GRAN HACKS CODE AND REBUILDS COMPUTERS THE WAY OTHER GRANDMAS BAKE COOKIES.
I BET OUR ESCAPED PRISONER IS HUNGRY. THERE'S FOOD IN THE FRIDGE. HELP YOURSELF.
OK, WHAT ARE WE EATING? GOT ANY FROZEN PIZZA BLASTERS? OR BURRITOS?
SLOW DOWN, SUPER CHEF. GOTTA WASH YOUR HANDS FIRST BEFORE WE EAT.
RUNNING WATER OVER YOUR HANDS IS NOT WASHING THEM, DEVIN.
SHEESH, YOU'RE WORSE THAN MY MOM.

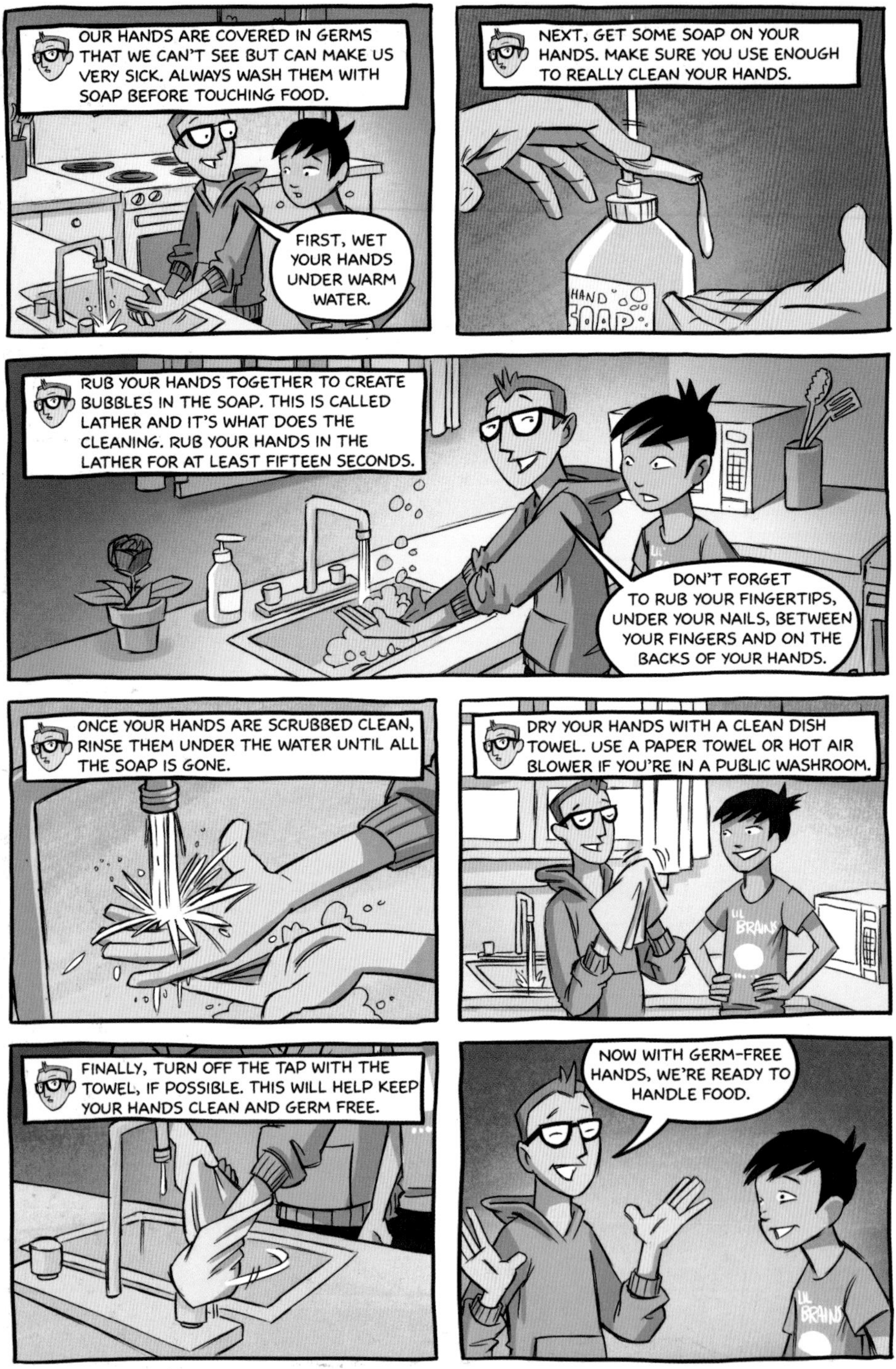
OUR HANDS ARE COVERED IN GERMS THAT WE CAN'T SEE BUT CAN MAKE US VERY SICK. ALWAYS WASH THEM WITH SOAP BEFORE TOUCHING FOOD.
FIRST, WET YOUR HANDS UNDER WARM WATER.
NEXT, GET SOME SOAP ON YOUR HANDS. MAKE SURE YOU USE ENOUGH TO REALLY CLEAN YOUR HANDS.
HAND SOAP
RUB YOUR HANDS TOGETHER TO CREATE BUBBLES IN THE SOAP. THIS IS CALLED LATHER AND IT'S WHAT DOES THE CLEANING. RUB YOUR HANDS IN THE LATHER FOR AT LEAST FIFTEEN SECONDS.
DON'T FORGET TO RUB YOUR FINGERTIPS, UNDER YOUR NAILS, BETWEEN YOUR FINGERS AND ON THE BACKS OF YOUR HANDS.
ONCE YOUR HANDS ARE SCRUBBED CLEAN, RINSE THEM UNDER THE WATER UNTIL ALL THE SOAP IS GONE.
DRY YOUR HANDS WITH A CLEAN DISH TOWEL. USE A PAPER TOWEL OR HOT AIR BLOWER IF YOU'RE IN A PUBLIC WASHROOM.
LIL BRAINS
FINALLY, TURN OFF THE TAP WITH THE TOWEL, IF POSSIBLE. THIS WILL HELP KEEP YOUR HANDS CLEAN AND GERM FREE.
NOW WITH GERM-FREE HANDS, WE'RE READY TO HANDLE FOOD.

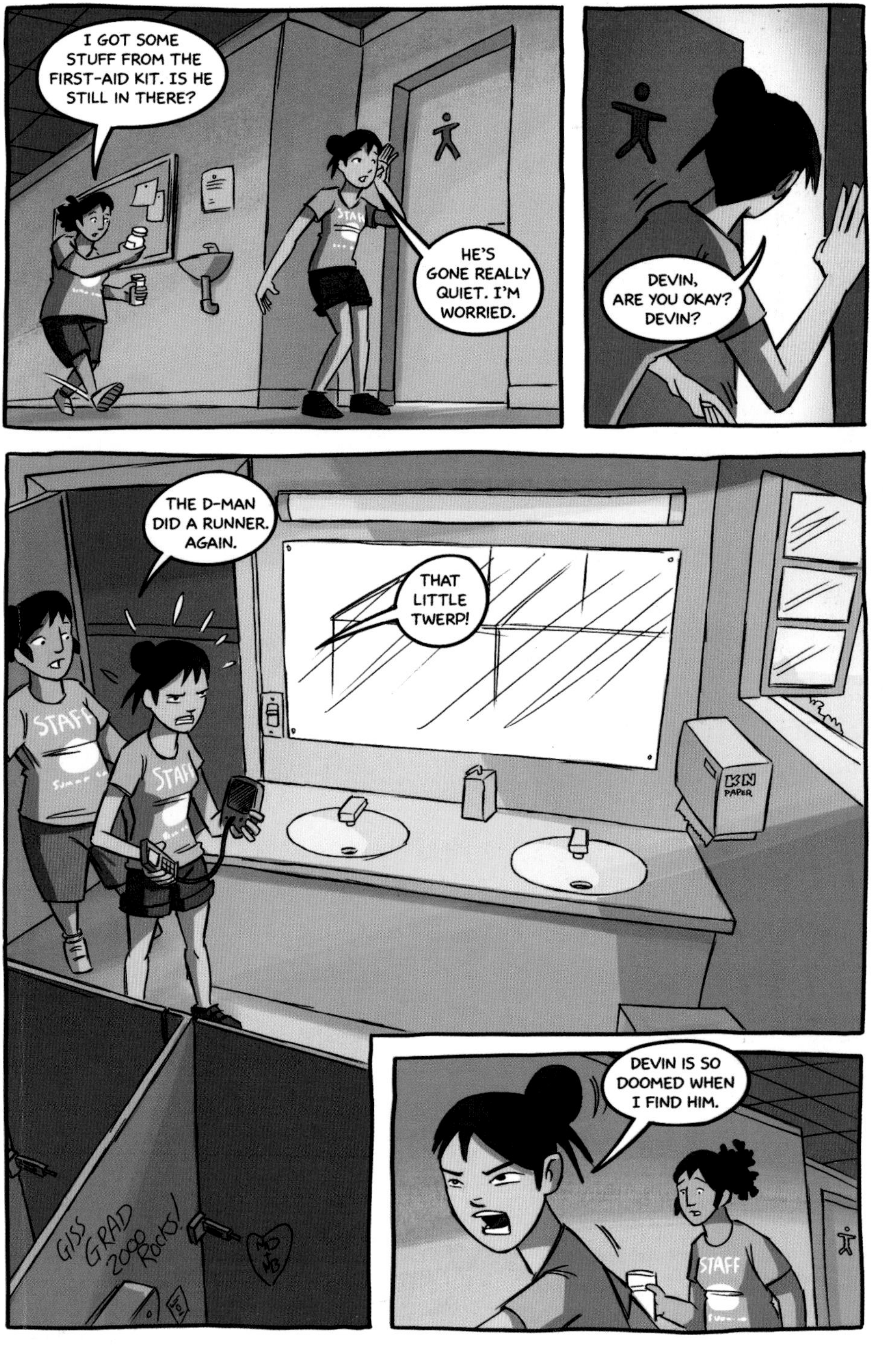
I GOT SOME STUFF FROM THE FIRST-AID KIT. IS HE STILL IN THERE?
HE'S GONE REALLY QUIET. I'M WORRIED.
DEVIN, ARE YOU OKAY? DEVIN?
THE D-MAN DID A RUNNER. AGAIN.
THAT LITTLE TWERP!
KN PAPER
GISS GRAD 2008 Rocks!
DEVIN IS SO DOOMED WHEN I FIND HIM.
STAFF

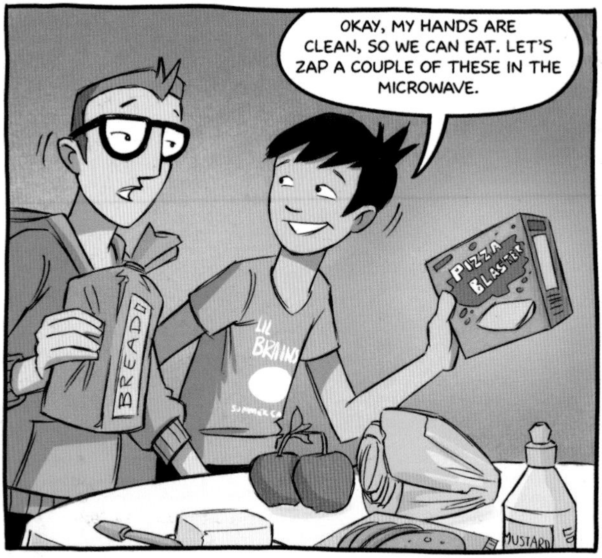
OKAY, MY HANDS ARE CLEAN, SO WE CAN EAT. LET'S ZAP A COUPLE OF THESE IN THE MICROWAVE.
BREAD
LIL BRAINS
PIZZA BLASTER
MUSTARD

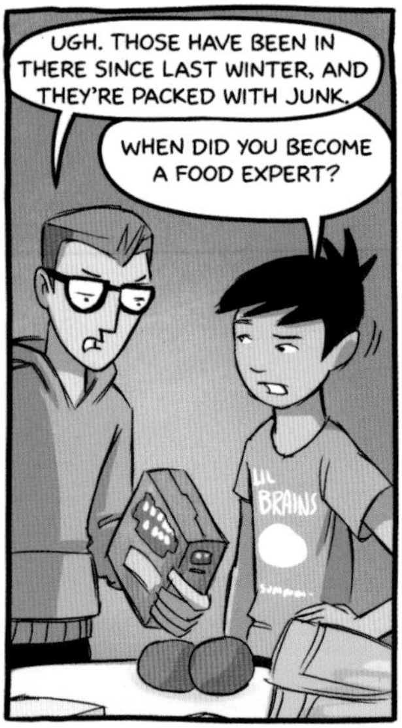
UGH. THOSE HAVE BEEN IN THERE SINCE LAST WINTER, AND THEY'RE PACKED WITH JUNK.
WHEN DID YOU BECOME A FOOD EXPERT?
LIL BRAINS

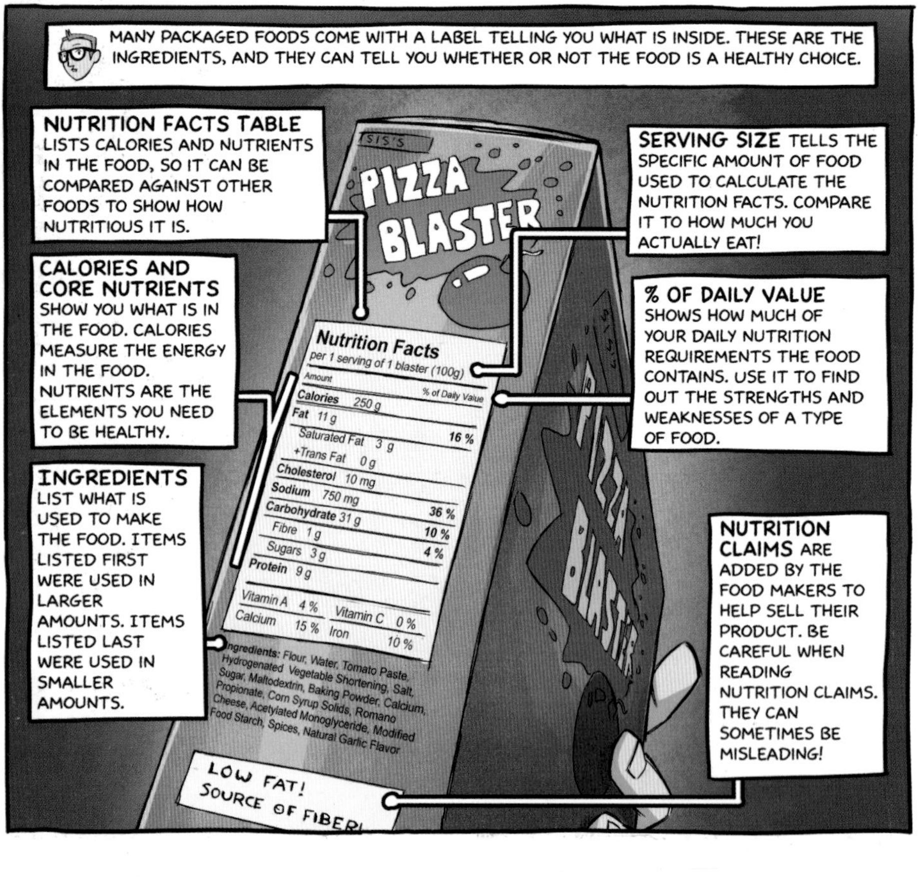
MANY PACKAGED FOODS COME WITH A LABEL TELLING YOU WHAT IS INSIDE. THESE ARE THE INGREDIENTS, AND THEY CAN TELL YOU WHETHER OR NOT THE FOOD IS A HEALTHY CHOICE.
NUTRITION FACTS TABLE LISTS CALORIES AND NUTRIENTS IN THE FOOD, SO IT CAN BE COMPARED AGAINST OTHER FOODS TO SHOW HOW NUTRITIOUS IT IS.
CALORIES AND CORE NUTRIENTS SHOW YOU WHAT IS IN THE FOOD. CALORIES MEASURE THE ENERGY IN THE FOOD. NUTRIENTS ARE THE ELEMENTS YOU NEED TO BE HEALTHY.
INGREDIENTS LIST WHAT IS USED TO MAKE THE FOOD. ITEMS LISTED FIRST WERE USED IN LARGER AMOUNTS. ITEMS LISTED LAST WERE USED IN SMALLER AMOUNTS.
SERVING SIZE TELLS THE SPECIFIC AMOUNT OF FOOD USED TO CALCULATE THE NUTRITION FACTS. COMPARE IT TO HOW MUCH YOU ACTUALLY EAT!
% OF DAILY VALUE SHOWS HOW MUCH OF YOUR DAILY NUTRITION REQUIREMENTS THE FOOD CONTAINS. USE IT TO FIND OUT THE STRENGTHS AND WEAKNESSES OF A TYPE OF FOOD.
NUTRITION CLAIMS ARE ADDED BY THE FOOD MAKERS TO HELP SELL THEIR PRODUCT. BE CAREFUL WHEN READING NUTRITION CLAIMS. THEY CAN SOMETIMES BE MISLEADING!
SIS'S
PIZZA BLASTER
Nutrition Facts
per 1 serving of 1 blaster (100g)
Amount
% of Daily Value
Calories 250 g
Fat 11 g
Saturated Fat 3 g 16 %
+Trans Fat 0 g
Cholesterol 10 mg
Sodium 750 mg
Carbohydrate 31 g 36 %
Fibre 1 g 10 %
Sugars 3 g 4 %
Protein 9 g
Vitamin A 4 % Vitamin C 0 %
Calcium 15 % Iron 10 %
Ingredients: Flour, Water, Tomato Paste, Hydrogenated Vegetable Shortening, Salt, Sugar, Maltodextrin, Baking Powder, Calcium, Propionate, Corn Syrup Solids, Romano Cheese, Acetylated Monoglyceride, Modified Food Starch, Spices, Natural Garlic Flavor
LOW FAT!
SOURCE OF FIBER!
PIZZA BLASTER

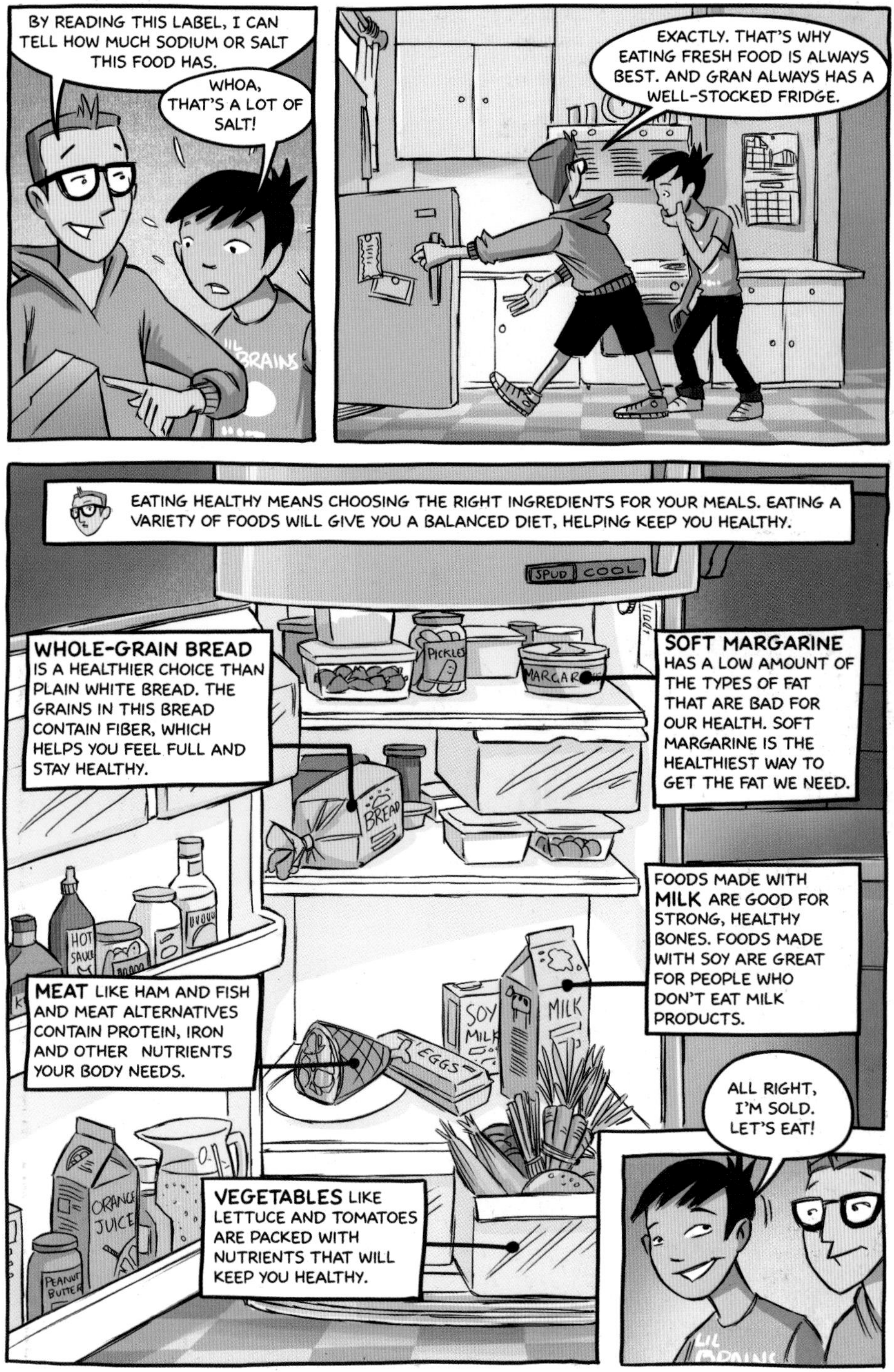

BY READING THIS LABEL, I CAN TELL HOW MUCH SODIUM OR SALT THIS FOOD HAS.
WHOA, THAT'S A LOT OF SALT!
LIL BRAINS
EXACTLY. THAT'S WHY EATING FRESH FOOD IS ALWAYS BEST. AND GRAN ALWAYS HAS A WELL-STOCKED FRIDGE.
EATING HEALTHY MEANS CHOOSING THE RIGHT INGREDIENTS FOR YOUR MEALS. EATING A VARIETY OF FOODS WILL GIVE YOU A BALANCED DIET, HELPING KEEP YOU HEALTHY.
SPUD COOL
WHOLE-GRAIN BREAD IS A HEALTHIER CHOICE THAN PLAIN WHITE BREAD. THE GRAINS IN THIS BREAD CONTAIN FIBER, WHICH HELPS YOU FEEL FULL AND STAY HEALTHY.
PICKLES
MARGAR
BREAD
SOFT MARGARINE HAS A LOW AMOUNT OF THE TYPES OF FAT THAT ARE BAD FOR OUR HEALTH. SOFT MARGARINE IS THE HEALTHIEST WAY TO GET THE FAT WE NEED.
HOT SAUCE
FOODS MADE WITH MILK ARE GOOD FOR STRONG, HEALTHY BONES. FOODS MADE WITH SOY ARE GREAT FOR PEOPLE WHO DON'T EAT MILK PRODUCTS.
SOY MILK
MILK
MEAT LIKE HAM AND FISH AND MEAT ALTERNATIVES CONTAIN PROTEIN, IRON AND OTHER NUTRIENTS YOUR BODY NEEDS.
EGGS
ALL RIGHT, I'M SOLD. LET'S EAT!
ORANGE JUICE
PEANUT BUTTER
VEGETABLES LIKE LETTUCE AND TOMATOES ARE PACKED WITH NUTRIENTS THAT WILL KEEP YOU HEALTHY.
LIL BRAINS

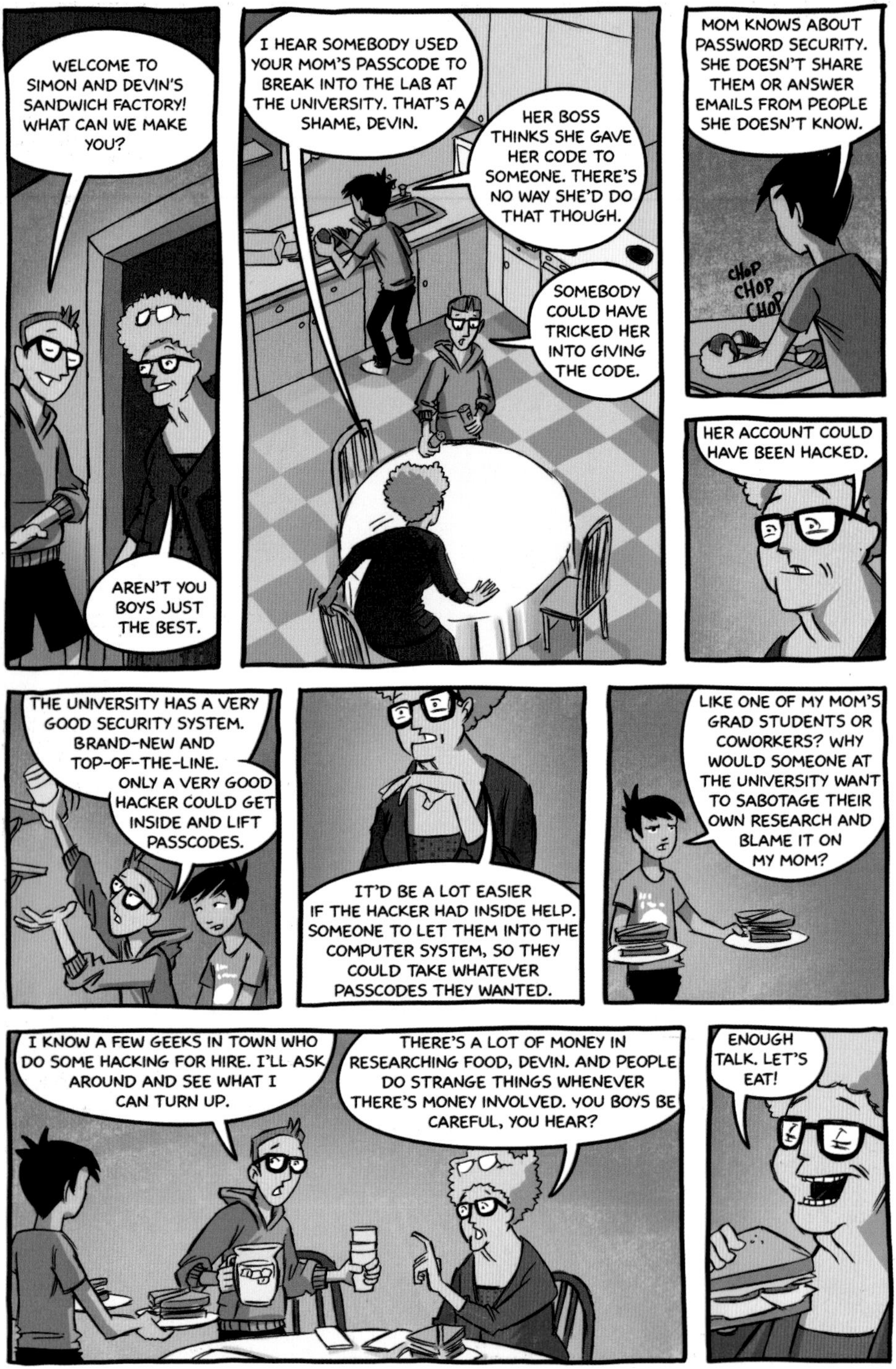
WELCOME TO SIMON AND DEVIN'S SANDWICH FACTORY! WHAT CAN WE MAKE YOU?
AREN'T YOU BOYS JUST THE BEST.
I HEAR SOMEBODY USED YOUR MOM'S PASSCODE TO BREAK INTO THE LAB AT THE UNIVERSITY. THAT'S A SHAME, DEVIN.
HER BOSS THINKS SHE GAVE HER CODE TO SOMEONE. THERE'S NO WAY SHE'D DO THAT THOUGH.
SOMEBODY COULD HAVE TRICKED HER INTO GIVING THE CODE.
MOM KNOWS ABOUT PASSWORD SECURITY. SHE DOESN'T SHARE THEM OR ANSWER EMAILS FROM PEOPLE SHE DOESN'T KNOW.
CHOP CHOP CHOP
HER ACCOUNT COULD HAVE BEEN HACKED.
THE UNIVERSITY HAS A VERY GOOD SECURITY SYSTEM. BRAND-NEW AND TOP-OF-THE-LINE.
ONLY A VERY GOOD HACKER COULD GET INSIDE AND LIFT PASSCODES.
IT'D BE A LOT EASIER IF THE HACKER HAD INSIDE HELP. SOMEONE TO LET THEM INTO THE COMPUTER SYSTEM, SO THEY COULD TAKE WHATEVER PASSCODES THEY WANTED.
LIKE ONE OF MY MOM'S GRAD STUDENTS OR COWORKERS? WHY WOULD SOMEONE AT THE UNIVERSITY WANT TO SABOTAGE THEIR OWN RESEARCH AND BLAME IT ON MY MOM?
I KNOW A FEW GEEKS IN TOWN WHO DO SOME HACKING FOR HIRE. I'LL ASK AROUND AND SEE WHAT I CAN TURN UP.
THERE'S A LOT OF MONEY IN RESEARCHING FOOD, DEVIN. AND PEOPLE DO STRANGE THINGS WHENEVER THERE'S MONEY INVOLVED. YOU BOYS BE CAREFUL, YOU HEAR?
ENOUGH TALK. LET'S EAT!

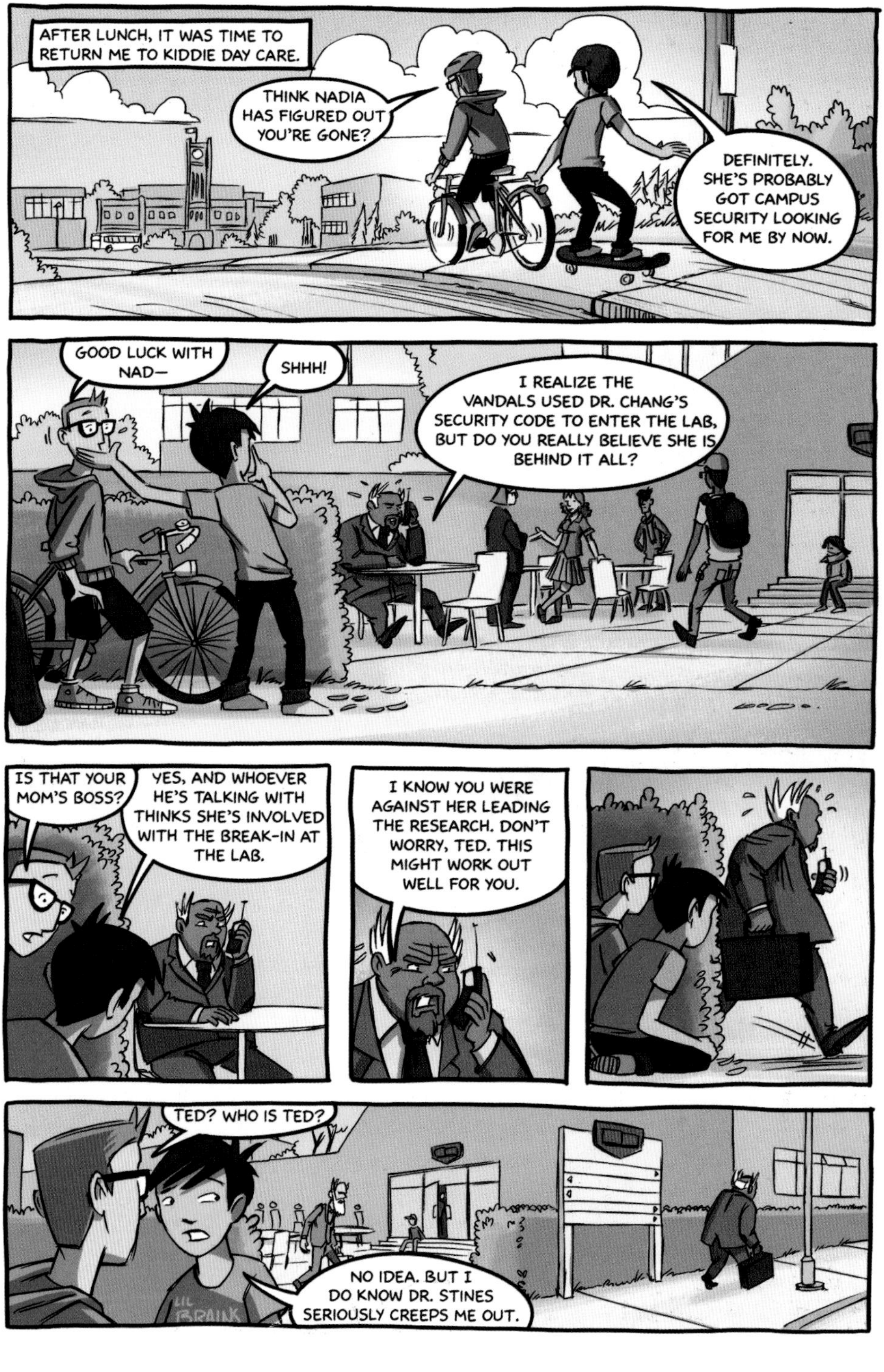
AFTER LUNCH, IT WAS TIME TO RETURN ME TO KIDDIE DAY CARE.
THINK NADIA HAS FIGURED OUT YOU'RE GONE?
DEFINITELY. SHE'S PROBABLY GOT CAMPUS SECURITY LOOKING FOR ME BY NOW.
GOOD LUCK WITH NAD—
SHHH!
I REALIZE THE VANDALS USED DR. CHANG'S SECURITY CODE TO ENTER THE LAB, BUT DO YOU REALLY BELIEVE SHE IS BEHIND IT ALL?
IS THAT YOUR MOM'S BOSS?
YES, AND WHOEVER HE'S TALKING WITH THINKS SHE'S INVOLVED WITH THE BREAK-IN AT THE LAB.
I KNOW YOU WERE AGAINST HER LEADING THE RESEARCH. DON'T WORRY, TED. THIS MIGHT WORK OUT WELL FOR YOU.
TED? WHO IS TED?
NO IDEA. BUT I DO KNOW DR. STINES SERIOUSLY CREEPS ME OUT.

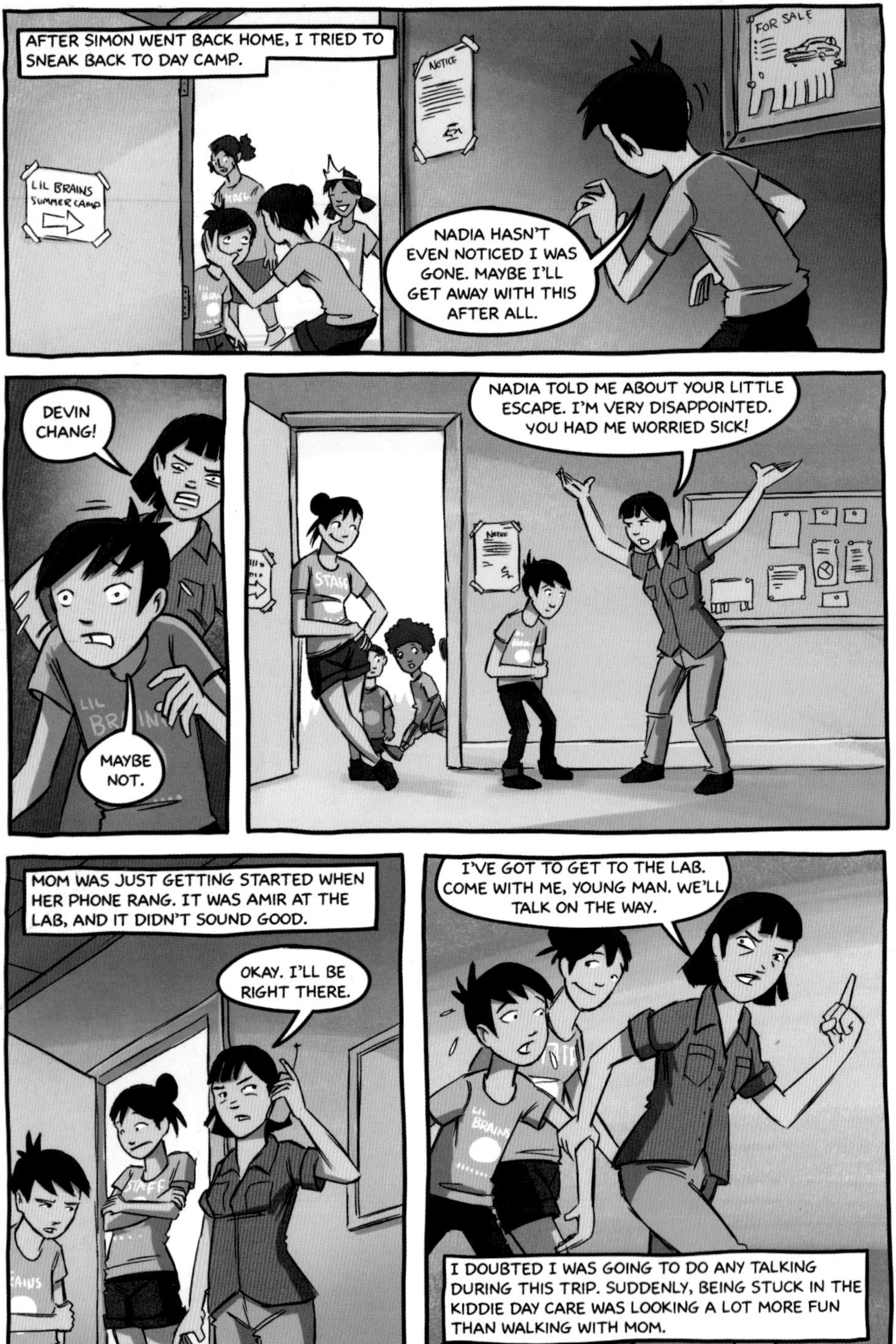
AFTER SIMON WENT BACK HOME, I TRIED TO SNEAK BACK TO DAY CAMP.
NOTICE
FOR SALE
LIL BRAINS SUMMER CAMP
NADIA HASN'T EVEN NOTICED I WAS GONE. MAYBE I'LL GET AWAY WITH THIS AFTER ALL.
DEVIN CHANG!
MAYBE NOT.
NADIA TOLD ME ABOUT YOUR LITTLE ESCAPE. I'M VERY DISAPPOINTED. YOU HAD ME WORRIED SICK!
MOM WAS JUST GETTING STARTED WHEN HER PHONE RANG. IT WAS AMIR AT THE LAB, AND IT DIDN'T SOUND GOOD.
OKAY. I'LL BE RIGHT THERE.
I'VE GOT TO GET TO THE LAB. COME WITH ME, YOUNG MAN. WE'LL TALK ON THE WAY.
I DOUBTED I WAS GOING TO DO ANY TALKING DURING THIS TRIP. SUDDENLY, BEING STUCK IN THE KIDDIE DAY CARE WAS LOOKING A LOT MORE FUN THAN WALKING WITH MOM.

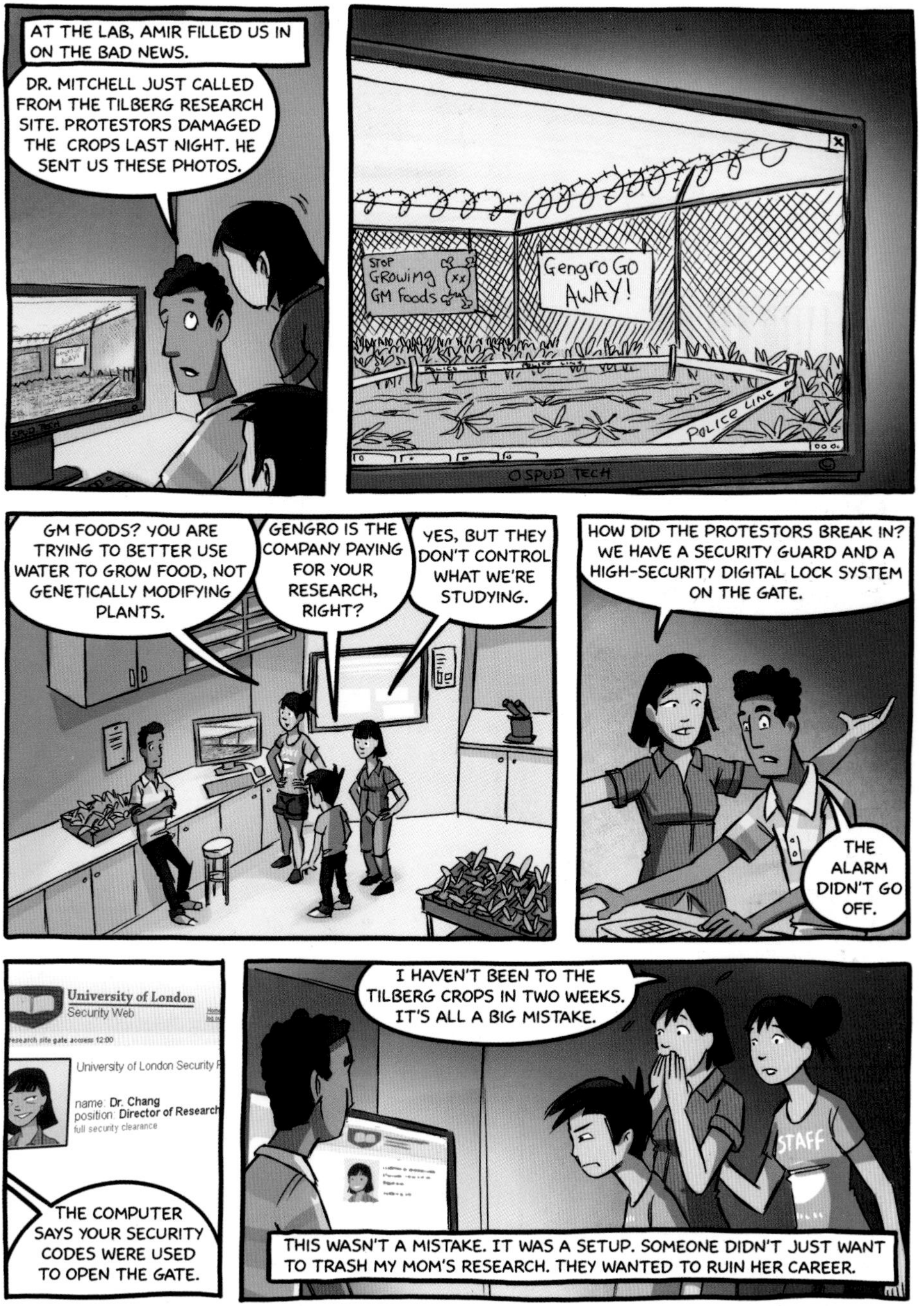
AT THE LAB, AMIR FILLED US IN ON THE BAD NEWS.
DR. MITCHELL JUST CALLED FROM THE TILBERG RESEARCH SITE. PROTESTORS DAMAGED THE CROPS LAST NIGHT. HE SENT US THESE PHOTOS.
STOP GROWING GM foods
Gengro Go AWAY!
POLICE LINE
SPUD TECH
GM FOODS? YOU ARE TRYING TO BETTER USE WATER TO GROW FOOD, NOT GENETICALLY MODIFYING PLANTS.
GENGRO IS THE COMPANY PAYING FOR YOUR RESEARCH, RIGHT?
YES, BUT THEY DON'T CONTROL WHAT WE'RE STUDYING.
HOW DID THE PROTESTORS BREAK IN? WE HAVE A SECURITY GUARD AND A HIGH-SECURITY DIGITAL LOCK SYSTEM ON THE GATE.
THE ALARM DIDN'T GO OFF.
University of London
Security Web
University of London Security
name: Dr. Chang
position: Director of Research
full security clearance
THE COMPUTER SAYS YOUR SECURITY CODES WERE USED TO OPEN THE GATE.
I HAVEN'T BEEN TO THE TILBERG CROPS IN TWO WEEKS. IT'S ALL A BIG MISTAKE.
STAFF
THIS WASN'T A MISTAKE. IT WAS A SETUP. SOMEONE DIDN'T JUST WANT TO TRASH MY MOM'S RESEARCH. THEY WANTED TO RUIN HER CAREER.

CHAPTER 3
ON THE ROAD

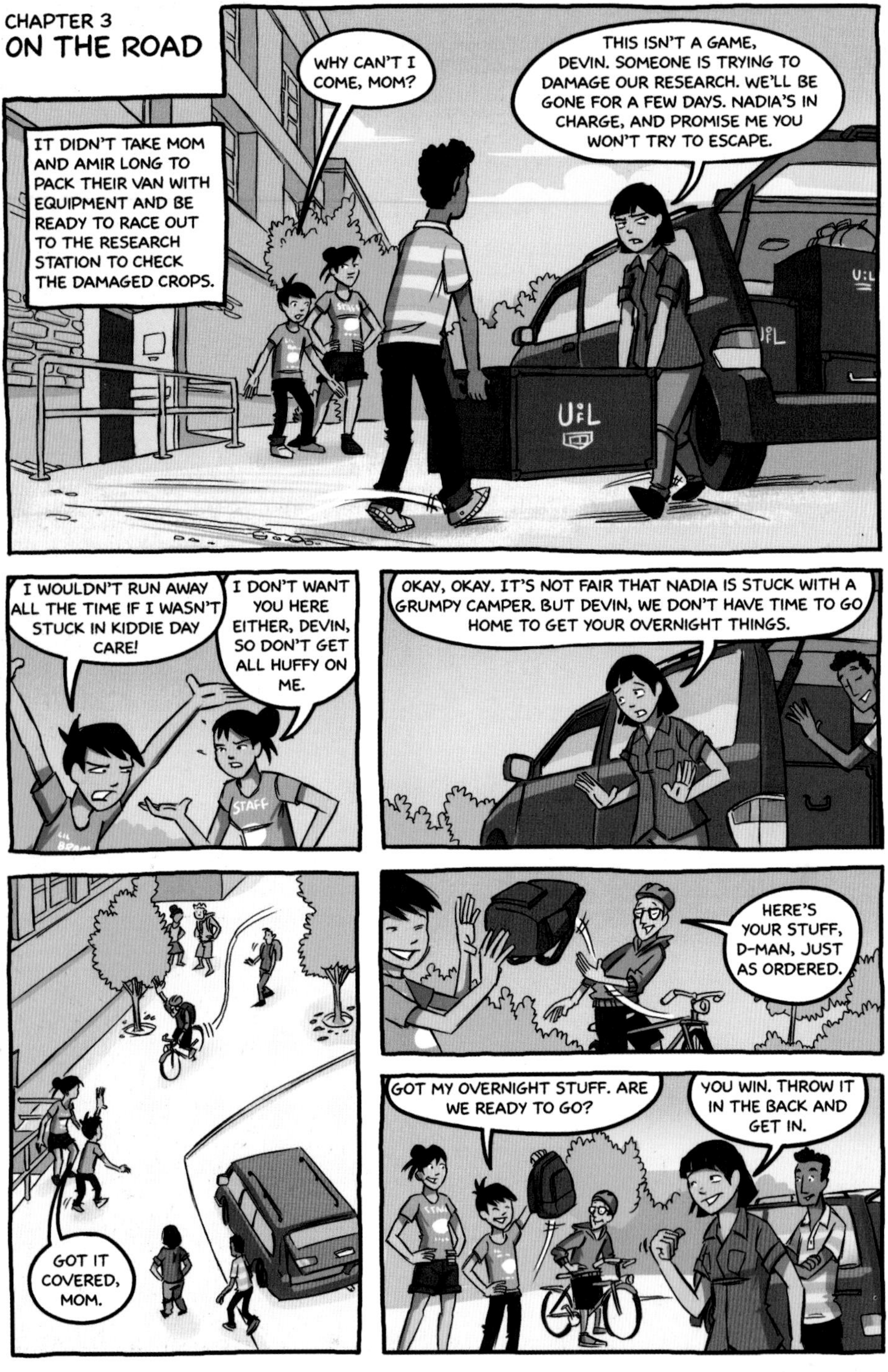
IT DIDN'T TAKE MOM AND AMIR LONG TO PACK THEIR VAN WITH EQUIPMENT AND BE READY TO RACE OUT TO THE RESEARCH STATION TO CHECK THE DAMAGED CROPS.
WHY CAN'T I COME, MOM?
THIS ISN'T A GAME, DEVIN. SOMEONE IS TRYING TO DAMAGE OUR RESEARCH. WE'LL BE GONE FOR A FEW DAYS. NADIA'S IN CHARGE, AND PROMISE ME YOU WON'T TRY TO ESCAPE.
U of L
I WOULDN'T RUN AWAY ALL THE TIME IF I WASN'T STUCK IN KIDDIE DAY CARE!
I DON'T WANT YOU HERE EITHER, DEVIN, SO DON'T GET ALL HUFFY ON ME.
STAFF
OKAY, OKAY. IT'S NOT FAIR THAT NADIA IS STUCK WITH A GRUMPY CAMPER. BUT DEVIN, WE DON'T HAVE TIME TO GO HOME TO GET YOUR OVERNIGHT THINGS.
GOT IT COVERED, MOM.
HERE'S YOUR STUFF, D-MAN, JUST AS ORDERED.
GOT MY OVERNIGHT STUFF. ARE WE READY TO GO?
YOU WIN. THROW IT IN THE BACK AND GET IN.

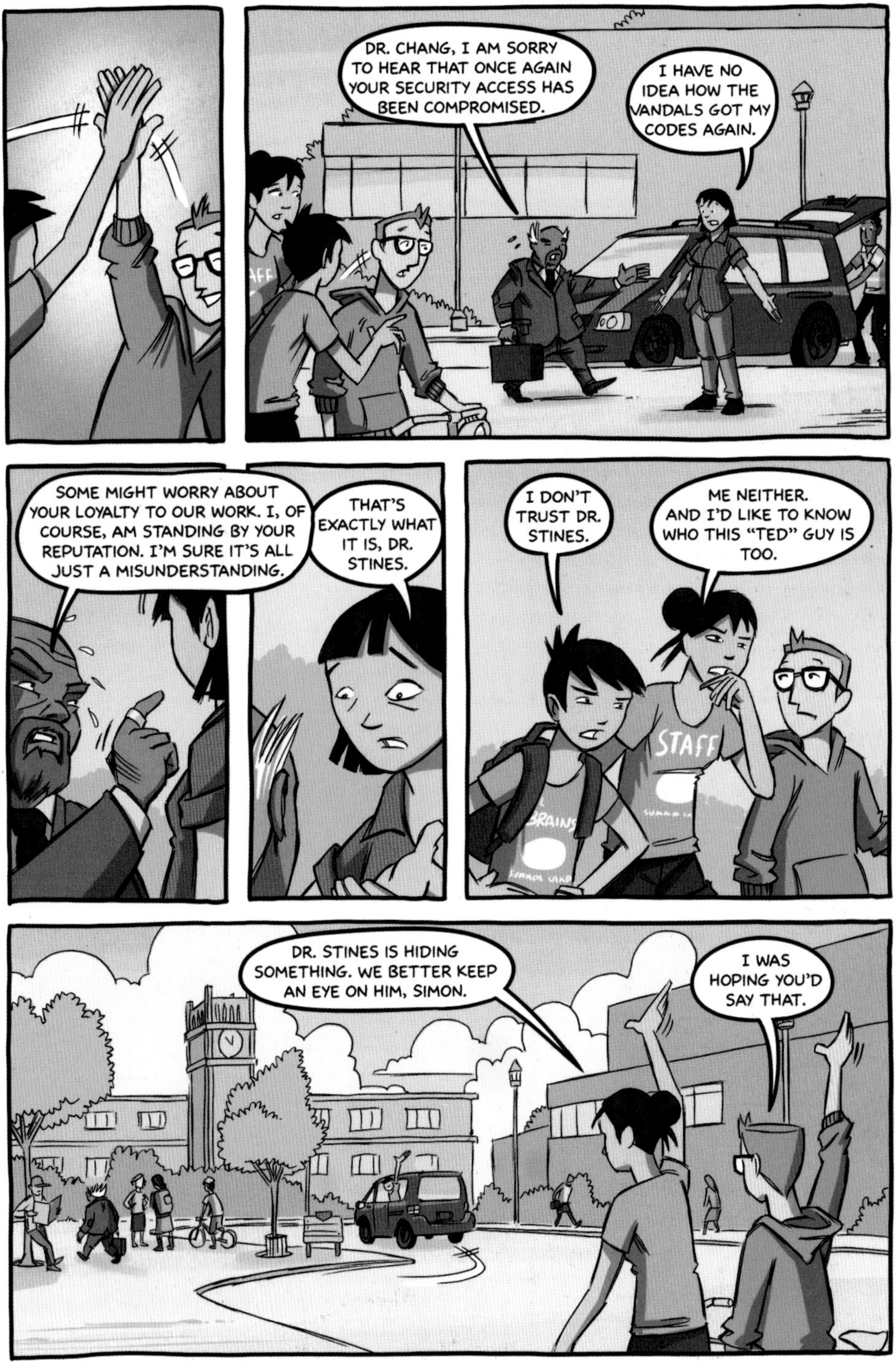
DR. CHANG, I AM SORRY TO HEAR THAT ONCE AGAIN YOUR SECURITY ACCESS HAS BEEN COMPROMISED.
I HAVE NO IDEA HOW THE VANDALS GOT MY CODES AGAIN.
SOME MIGHT WORRY ABOUT YOUR LOYALTY TO OUR WORK. I, OF COURSE, AM STANDING BY YOUR REPUTATION. I'M SURE IT'S ALL JUST A MISUNDERSTANDING.
THAT'S EXACTLY WHAT IT IS, DR. STINES.
I DON'T TRUST DR. STINES.
ME NEITHER. AND I'D LIKE TO KNOW WHO THIS "TED" GUY IS TOO.
STAFF
DR. STINES IS HIDING SOMETHING. WE BETTER KEEP AN EYE ON HIM, SIMON.
I WAS HOPING YOU'D SAY THAT.

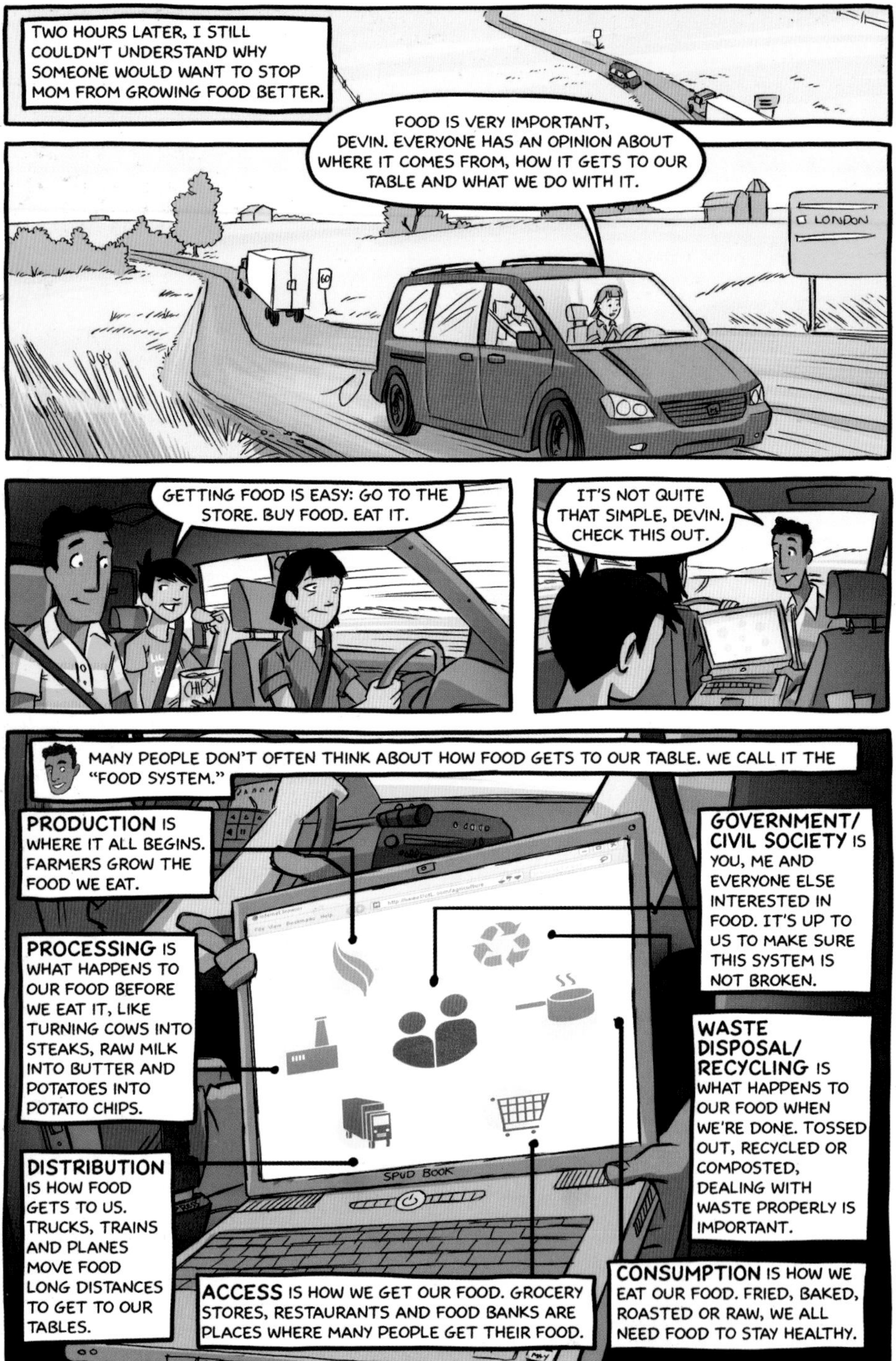

TWO HOURS LATER, I STILL COULDN'T UNDERSTAND WHY SOMEONE WOULD WANT TO STOP MOM FROM GROWING FOOD BETTER.
FOOD IS VERY IMPORTANT, DEVIN. EVERYONE HAS AN OPINION ABOUT WHERE IT COMES FROM, HOW IT GETS TO OUR TABLE AND WHAT WE DO WITH IT.
LONDON
GETTING FOOD IS EASY: GO TO THE STORE. BUY FOOD. EAT IT.
IT'S NOT QUITE THAT SIMPLE, DEVIN. CHECK THIS OUT.
MANY PEOPLE DON'T OFTEN THINK ABOUT HOW FOOD GETS TO OUR TABLE. WE CALL IT THE "FOOD SYSTEM."
PRODUCTION IS WHERE IT ALL BEGINS. FARMERS GROW THE FOOD WE EAT.
PROCESSING IS WHAT HAPPENS TO OUR FOOD BEFORE WE EAT IT, LIKE TURNING COWS INTO STEAKS, RAW MILK INTO BUTTER AND POTATOES INTO POTATO CHIPS.
DISTRIBUTION IS HOW FOOD GETS TO US. TRUCKS, TRAINS AND PLANES MOVE FOOD LONG DISTANCES TO GET TO OUR TABLES.
ACCESS IS HOW WE GET OUR FOOD. GROCERY STORES, RESTAURANTS AND FOOD BANKS ARE PLACES WHERE MANY PEOPLE GET THEIR FOOD.
CONSUMPTION IS HOW WE EAT OUR FOOD. FRIED, BAKED, ROASTED OR RAW, WE ALL NEED FOOD TO STAY HEALTHY.
WASTE DISPOSAL/ RECYCLING IS WHAT HAPPENS TO OUR FOOD WHEN WE'RE DONE. TOSSED OUT, RECYCLED OR COMPOSTED, DEALING WITH WASTE PROPERLY IS IMPORTANT.
GOVERNMENT/ CIVIL SOCIETY IS YOU, ME AND EVERYONE ELSE INTERESTED IN FOOD. IT'S UP TO US TO MAKE SURE THIS SYSTEM IS NOT BROKEN.
SPUD BOOK

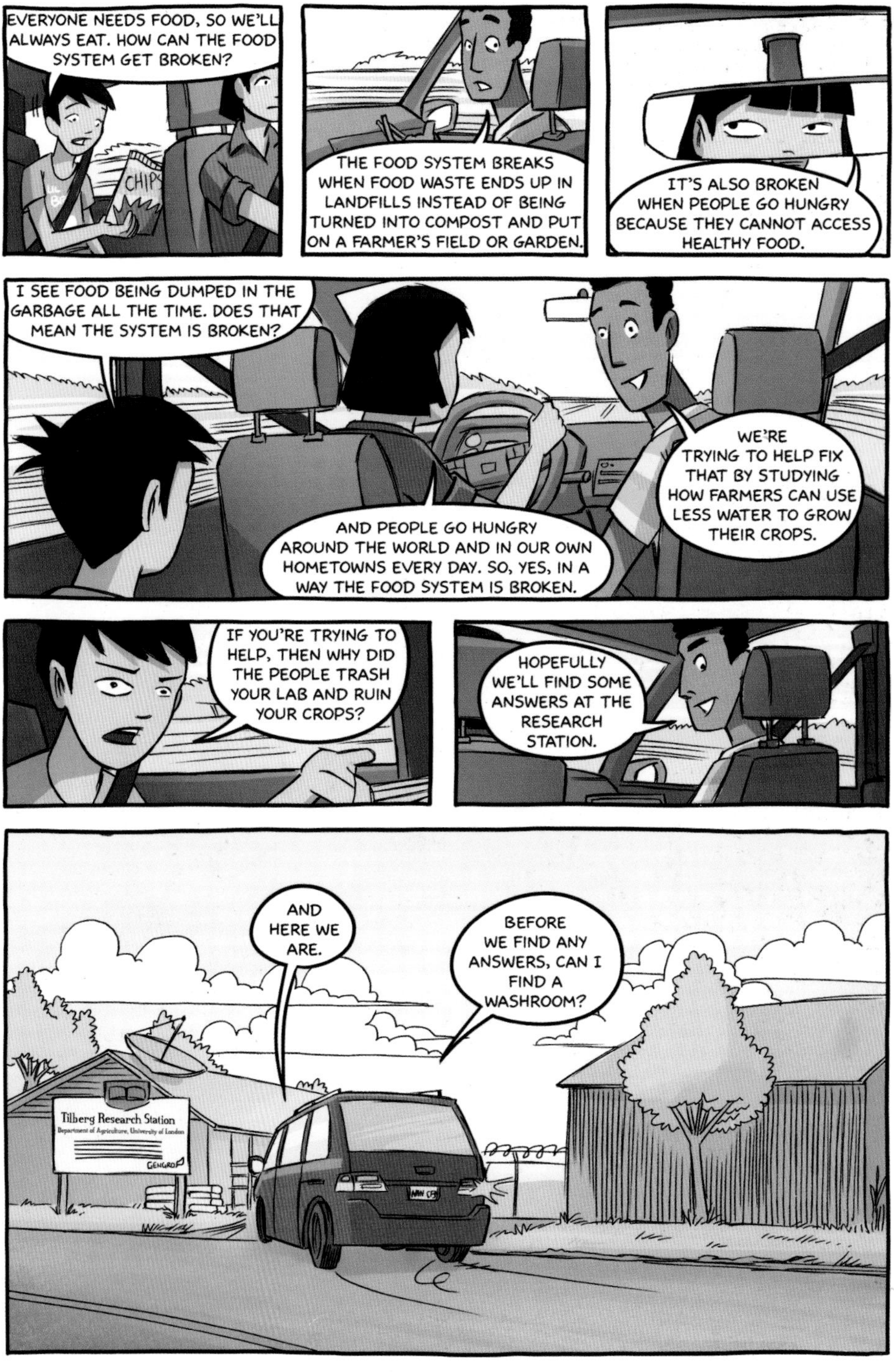
EVERYONE NEEDS FOOD, SO WE'LL ALWAYS EAT. HOW CAN THE FOOD SYSTEM GET BROKEN?
CHIPS
THE FOOD SYSTEM BREAKS WHEN FOOD WASTE ENDS UP IN LANDFILLS INSTEAD OF BEING TURNED INTO COMPOST AND PUT ON A FARMER'S FIELD OR GARDEN.
IT'S ALSO BROKEN WHEN PEOPLE GO HUNGRY BECAUSE THEY CANNOT ACCESS HEALTHY FOOD.
I SEE FOOD BEING DUMPED IN THE GARBAGE ALL THE TIME. DOES THAT MEAN THE SYSTEM IS BROKEN?
AND PEOPLE GO HUNGRY AROUND THE WORLD AND IN OUR OWN HOMETOWNS EVERY DAY. SO, YES, IN A WAY THE FOOD SYSTEM IS BROKEN.
WE'RE TRYING TO HELP FIX THAT BY STUDYING HOW FARMERS CAN USE LESS WATER TO GROW THEIR CROPS.
IF YOU'RE TRYING TO HELP, THEN WHY DID THE PEOPLE TRASH YOUR LAB AND RUIN YOUR CROPS?
HOPEFULLY WE'LL FIND SOME ANSWERS AT THE RESEARCH STATION.
AND HERE WE ARE.
BEFORE WE FIND ANY ANSWERS, CAN I FIND A WASHROOM?
Tilberg Research Station
Department of Agriculture, University of London
GENGRO

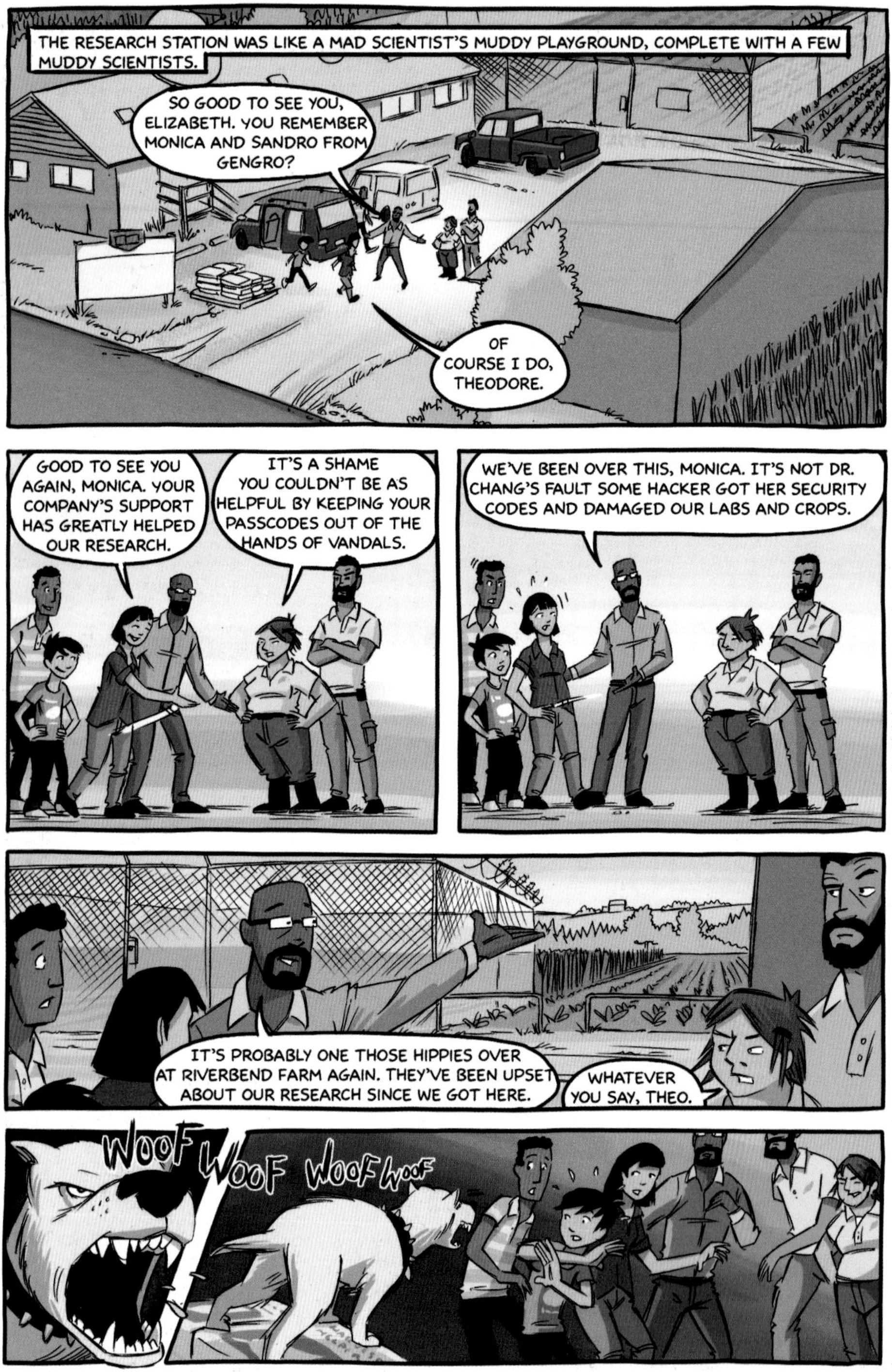
THE RESEARCH STATION WAS LIKE A MAD SCIENTIST'S MUDDY PLAYGROUND, COMPLETE WITH A FEW MUDDY SCIENTISTS.
SO GOOD TO SEE YOU, ELIZABETH. YOU REMEMBER MONICA AND SANDRO FROM GENGRO?
OF COURSE I DO, THEODORE.
GOOD TO SEE YOU AGAIN, MONICA. YOUR COMPANY'S SUPPORT HAS GREATLY HELPED OUR RESEARCH.
IT'S A SHAME YOU COULDN'T BE AS HELPFUL BY KEEPING YOUR PASSCODES OUT OF THE HANDS OF VANDALS.
WE'VE BEEN OVER THIS, MONICA. IT'S NOT DR. CHANG'S FAULT SOME HACKER GOT HER SECURITY CODES AND DAMAGED OUR LABS AND CROPS.
IT'S PROBABLY ONE THOSE HIPPIES OVER AT RIVERBEND FARM AGAIN. THEY'VE BEEN UPSET ABOUT OUR RESEARCH SINCE WE GOT HERE.
WHATEVER YOU SAY, THEO.
WOOF WOOF WOOF WOOF

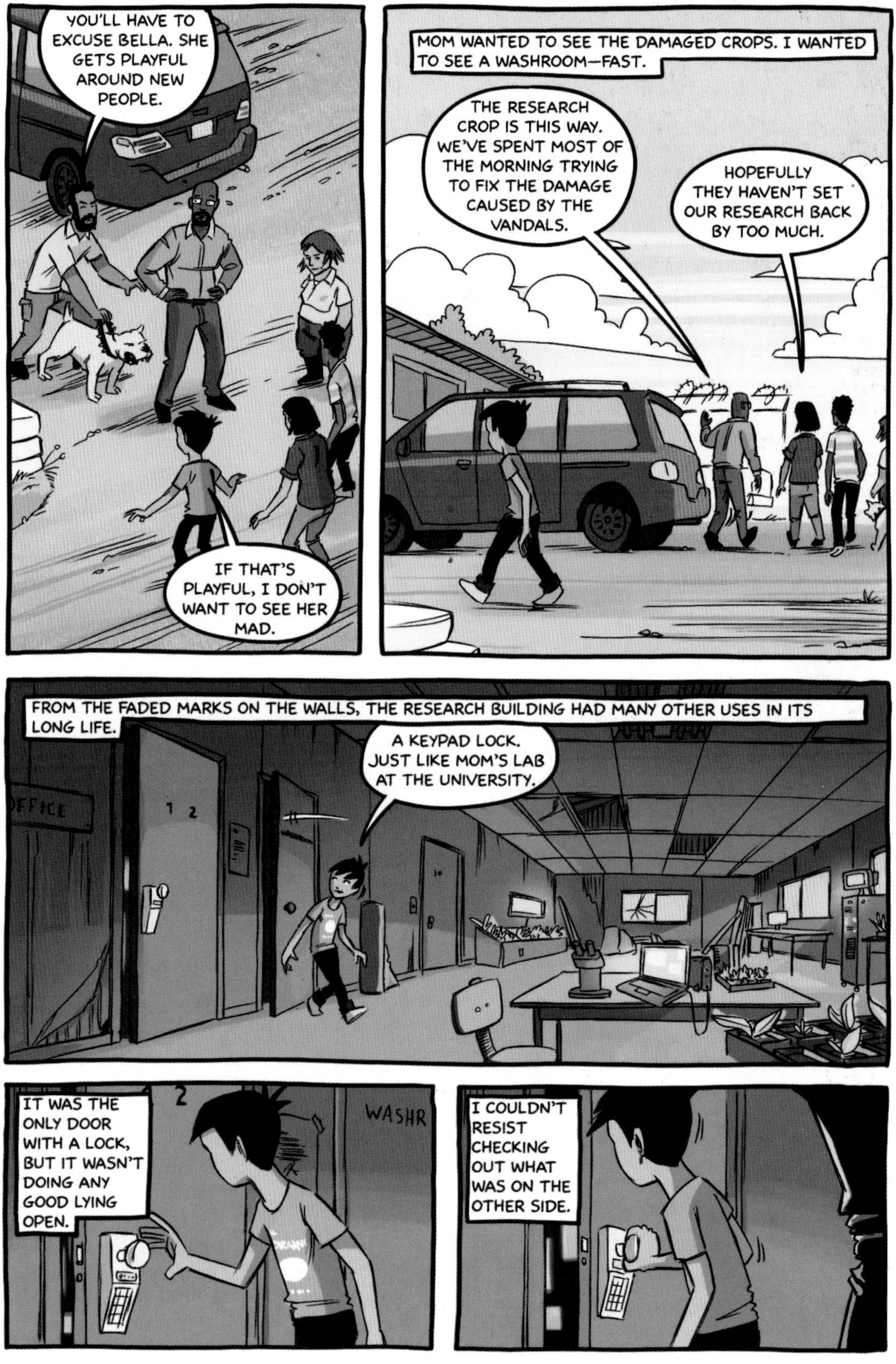

YOU'LL HAVE TO EXCUSE BELLA. SHE GETS PLAYFUL AROUND NEW PEOPLE.
IF THAT'S PLAYFUL, I DON'T WANT TO SEE HER MAD.
MOM WANTED TO SEE THE DAMAGED CROPS. I WANTED TO SEE A WASHROOM—FAST.
THE RESEARCH CROP IS THIS WAY. WE'VE SPENT MOST OF THE MORNING TRYING TO FIX THE DAMAGE CAUSED BY THE VANDALS.
HOPEFULLY THEY HAVEN'T SET OUR RESEARCH BACK BY TOO MUCH.
FROM THE FADED MARKS ON THE WALLS, THE RESEARCH BUILDING HAD MANY OTHER USES IN ITS LONG LIFE.
A KEYPAD LOCK. JUST LIKE MOM'S LAB AT THE UNIVERSITY.
IT WAS THE ONLY DOOR WITH A LOCK, BUT IT WASN'T DOING ANY GOOD LYING OPEN.
WASHR
I COULDN'T RESIST CHECKING OUT WHAT WAS ON THE OTHER SIDE.

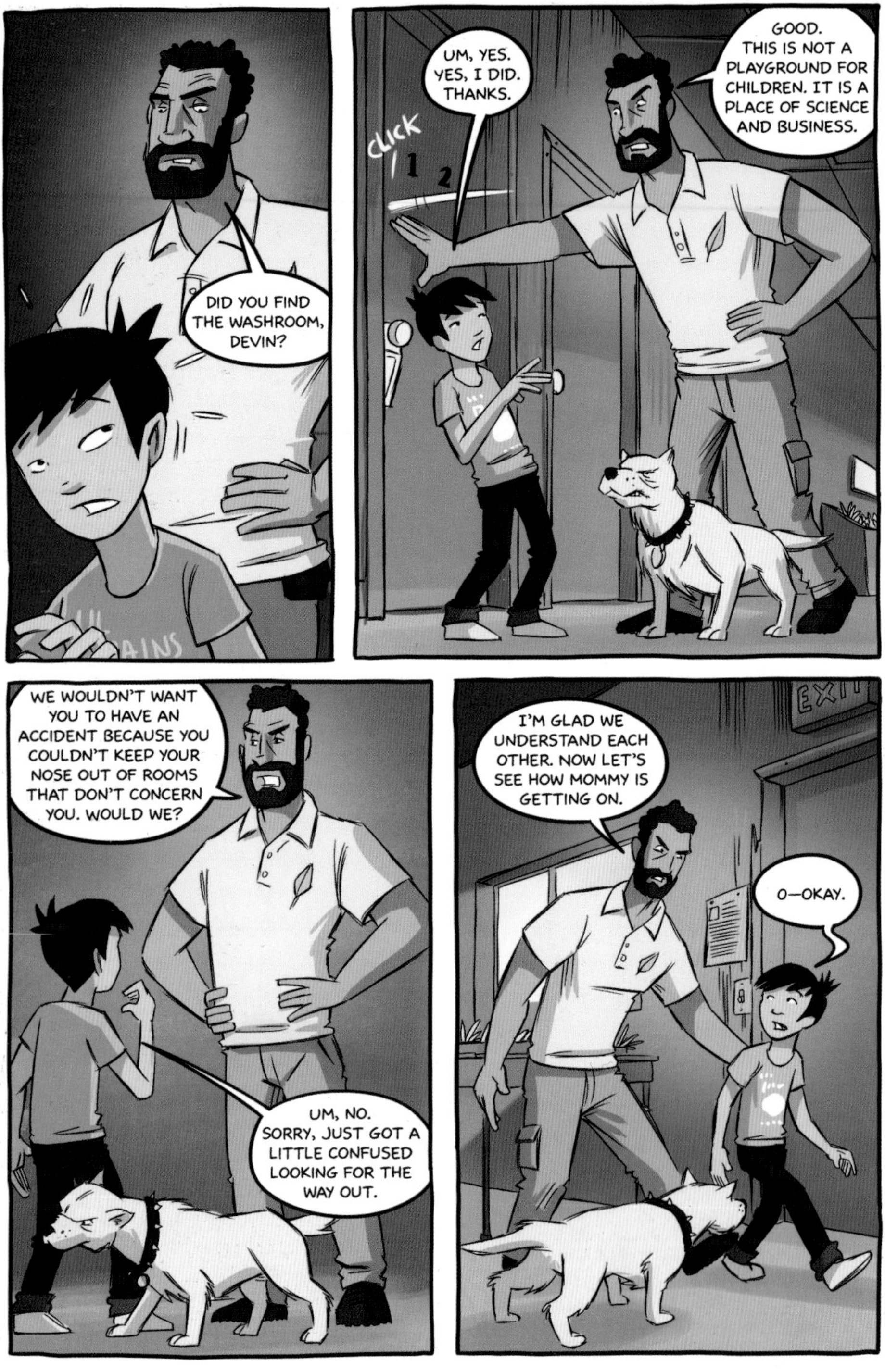
DID YOU FIND THE WASHROOM, DEVIN?
UM, YES. YES, I DID. THANKS.
CLICK
1
2
GOOD. THIS IS NOT A PLAYGROUND FOR CHILDREN. IT IS A PLACE OF SCIENCE AND BUSINESS.
WE WOULDN'T WANT YOU TO HAVE AN ACCIDENT BECAUSE YOU COULDN'T KEEP YOUR NOSE OUT OF ROOMS THAT DON'T CONCERN YOU. WOULD WE?
UM, NO. SORRY, JUST GOT A LITTLE CONFUSED LOOKING FOR THE WAY OUT.
I'M GLAD WE UNDERSTAND EACH OTHER. NOW LET'S SEE HOW MOMMY IS GETTING ON.
O—OKAY.

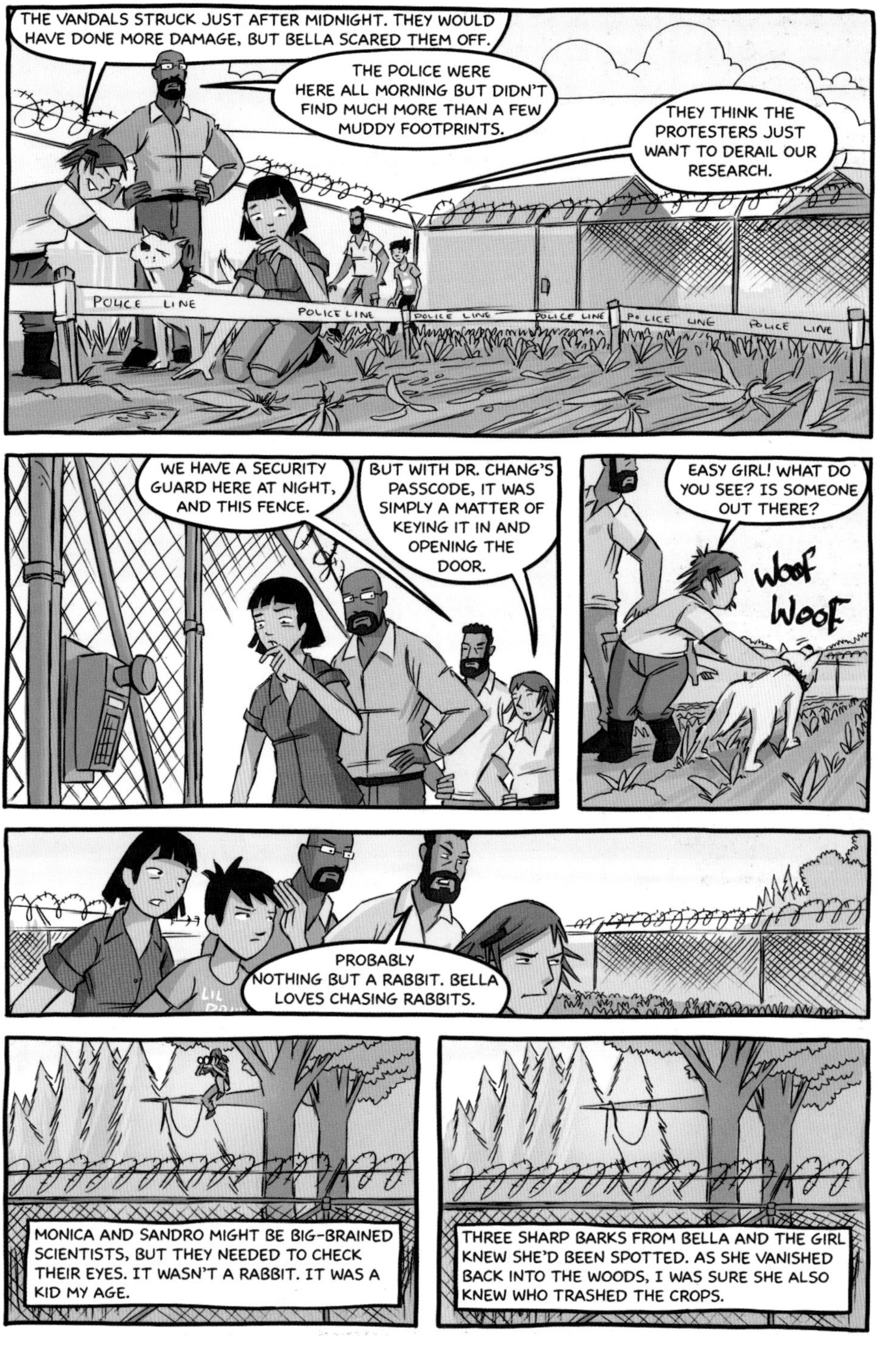

THE VANDALS STRUCK JUST AFTER MIDNIGHT. THEY WOULD HAVE DONE MORE DAMAGE, BUT BELLA SCARED THEM OFF.
THE POLICE WERE HERE ALL MORNING BUT DIDN'T FIND MUCH MORE THAN A FEW MUDDY FOOTPRINTS.
THEY THINK THE PROTESTERS JUST WANT TO DERAIL OUR RESEARCH.
POLICE LINE
POLICE LINE
POLICE LINE
POLICE LINE
POLICE LINE
POLICE LINE
WE HAVE A SECURITY GUARD HERE AT NIGHT, AND THIS FENCE.
BUT WITH DR. CHANG'S PASSCODE, IT WAS SIMPLY A MATTER OF KEYING IT IN AND OPENING THE DOOR.
EASY GIRL! WHAT DO YOU SEE? IS SOMEONE OUT THERE?
WOOF
WOOF
PROBABLY NOTHING BUT A RABBIT. BELLA LOVES CHASING RABBITS.
MONICA AND SANDRO MIGHT BE BIG-BRAINED SCIENTISTS, BUT THEY NEEDED TO CHECK THEIR EYES. IT WASN'T A RABBIT. IT WAS A KID MY AGE.
THREE SHARP BARKS FROM BELLA AND THE GIRL KNEW SHE'D BEEN SPOTTED. AS SHE VANISHED BACK INTO THE WOODS, I WAS SURE SHE ALSO KNEW WHO TRASHED THE CROPS.

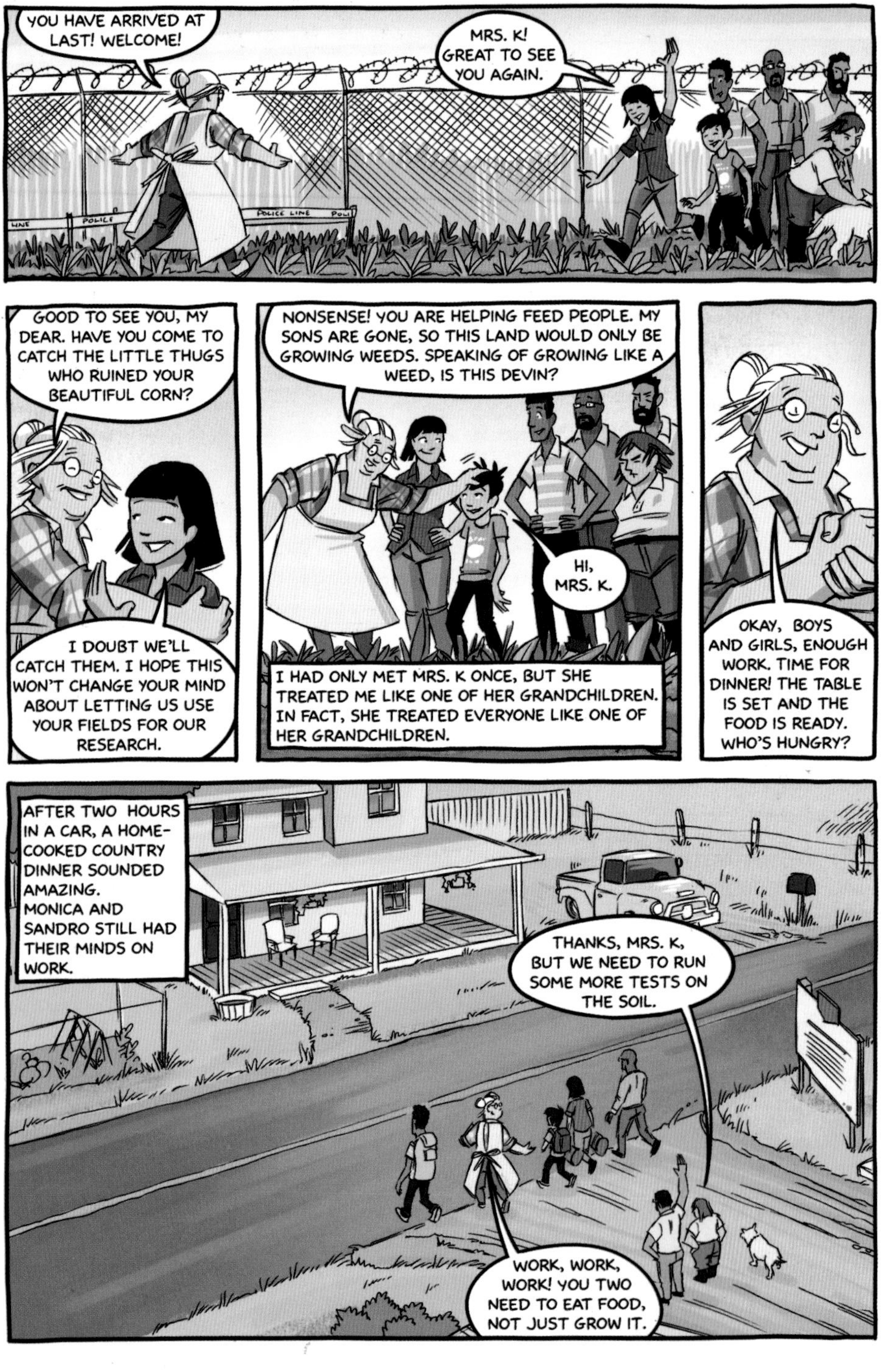
YOU HAVE ARRIVED AT LAST! WELCOME!
MRS. K! GREAT TO SEE YOU AGAIN.
GOOD TO SEE YOU, MY DEAR. HAVE YOU COME TO CATCH THE LITTLE THUGS WHO RUINED YOUR BEAUTIFUL CORN?
I DOUBT WE'LL CATCH THEM. I HOPE THIS WON'T CHANGE YOUR MIND ABOUT LETTING US USE YOUR FIELDS FOR OUR RESEARCH.
NONSENSE! YOU ARE HELPING FEED PEOPLE. MY SONS ARE GONE, SO THIS LAND WOULD ONLY BE GROWING WEEDS. SPEAKING OF GROWING LIKE A WEED, IS THIS DEVIN?
HI, MRS. K.
I HAD ONLY MET MRS. K ONCE, BUT SHE TREATED ME LIKE ONE OF HER GRANDCHILDREN. IN FACT, SHE TREATED EVERYONE LIKE ONE OF HER GRANDCHILDREN.
OKAY, BOYS AND GIRLS, ENOUGH WORK. TIME FOR DINNER! THE TABLE IS SET AND THE FOOD IS READY. WHO'S HUNGRY?
AFTER TWO HOURS IN A CAR, A HOME-COOKED COUNTRY DINNER SOUNDED AMAZING. MONICA AND SANDRO STILL HAD THEIR MINDS ON WORK.
THANKS, MRS. K, BUT WE NEED TO RUN SOME MORE TESTS ON THE SOIL.
WORK, WORK, WORK! YOU TWO NEED TO EAT FOOD, NOT JUST GROW IT.

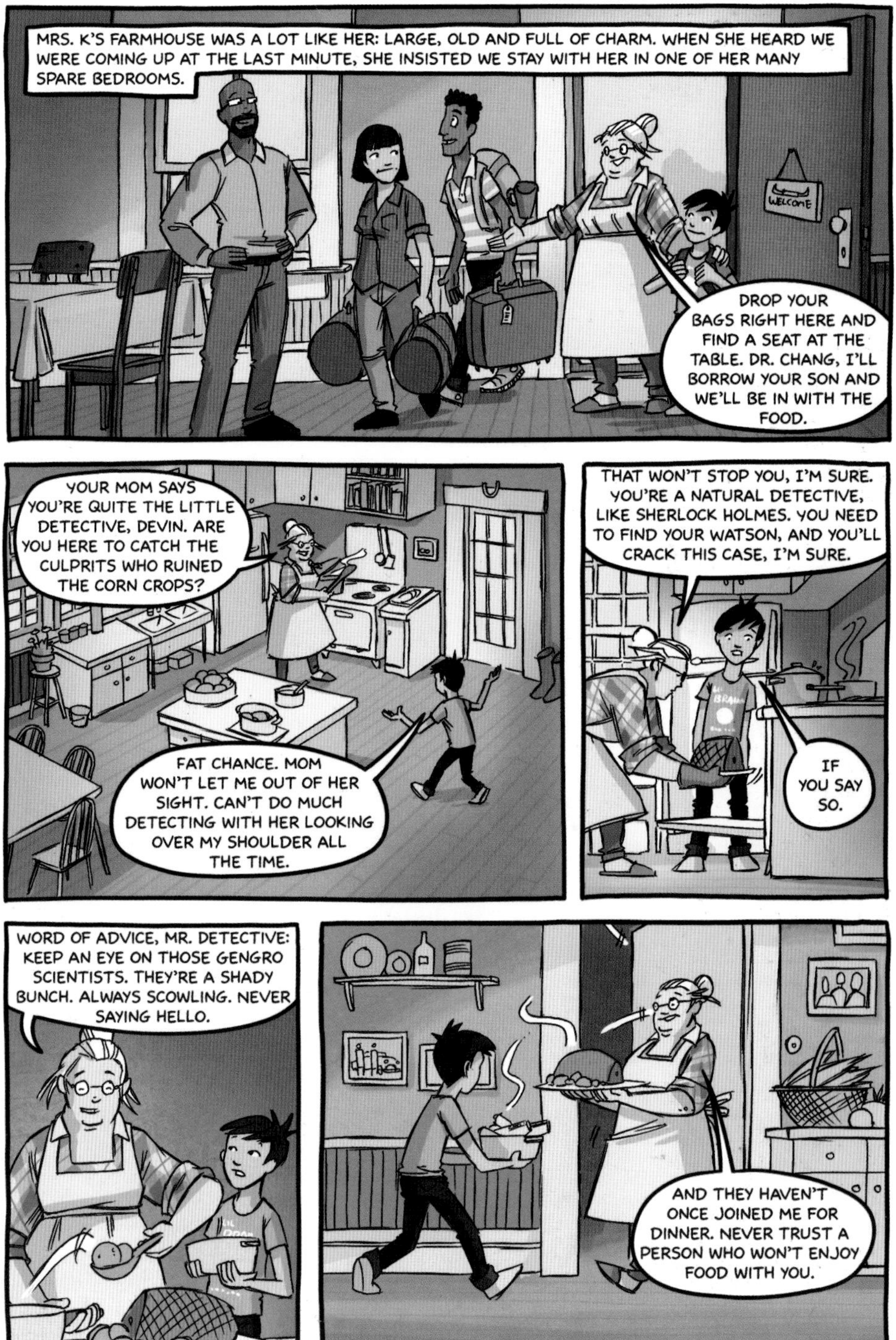
MRS. K'S FARMHOUSE WAS A LOT LIKE HER: LARGE, OLD AND FULL OF CHARM. WHEN SHE HEARD WE WERE COMING UP AT THE LAST MINUTE, SHE INSISTED WE STAY WITH HER IN ONE OF HER MANY SPARE BEDROOMS.
WELCOME
DROP YOUR BAGS RIGHT HERE AND FIND A SEAT AT THE TABLE. DR. CHANG, I'LL BORROW YOUR SON AND WE'LL BE IN WITH THE FOOD.
YOUR MOM SAYS YOU'RE QUITE THE LITTLE DETECTIVE, DEVIN. ARE YOU HERE TO CATCH THE CULPRITS WHO RUINED THE CORN CROPS?
FAT CHANCE. MOM WON'T LET ME OUT OF HER SIGHT. CAN'T DO MUCH DETECTING WITH HER LOOKING OVER MY SHOULDER ALL THE TIME.
THAT WON'T STOP YOU, I'M SURE. YOU'RE A NATURAL DETECTIVE, LIKE SHERLOCK HOLMES. YOU NEED TO FIND YOUR WATSON, AND YOU'LL CRACK THIS CASE, I'M SURE.
IF YOU SAY SO.
WORD OF ADVICE, MR. DETECTIVE: KEEP AN EYE ON THOSE GENGRO SCIENTISTS. THEY'RE A SHADY BUNCH. ALWAYS SCOWLING. NEVER SAYING HELLO.
AND THEY HAVEN'T ONCE JOINED ME FOR DINNER. NEVER TRUST A PERSON WHO WON'T ENJOY FOOD WITH YOU.

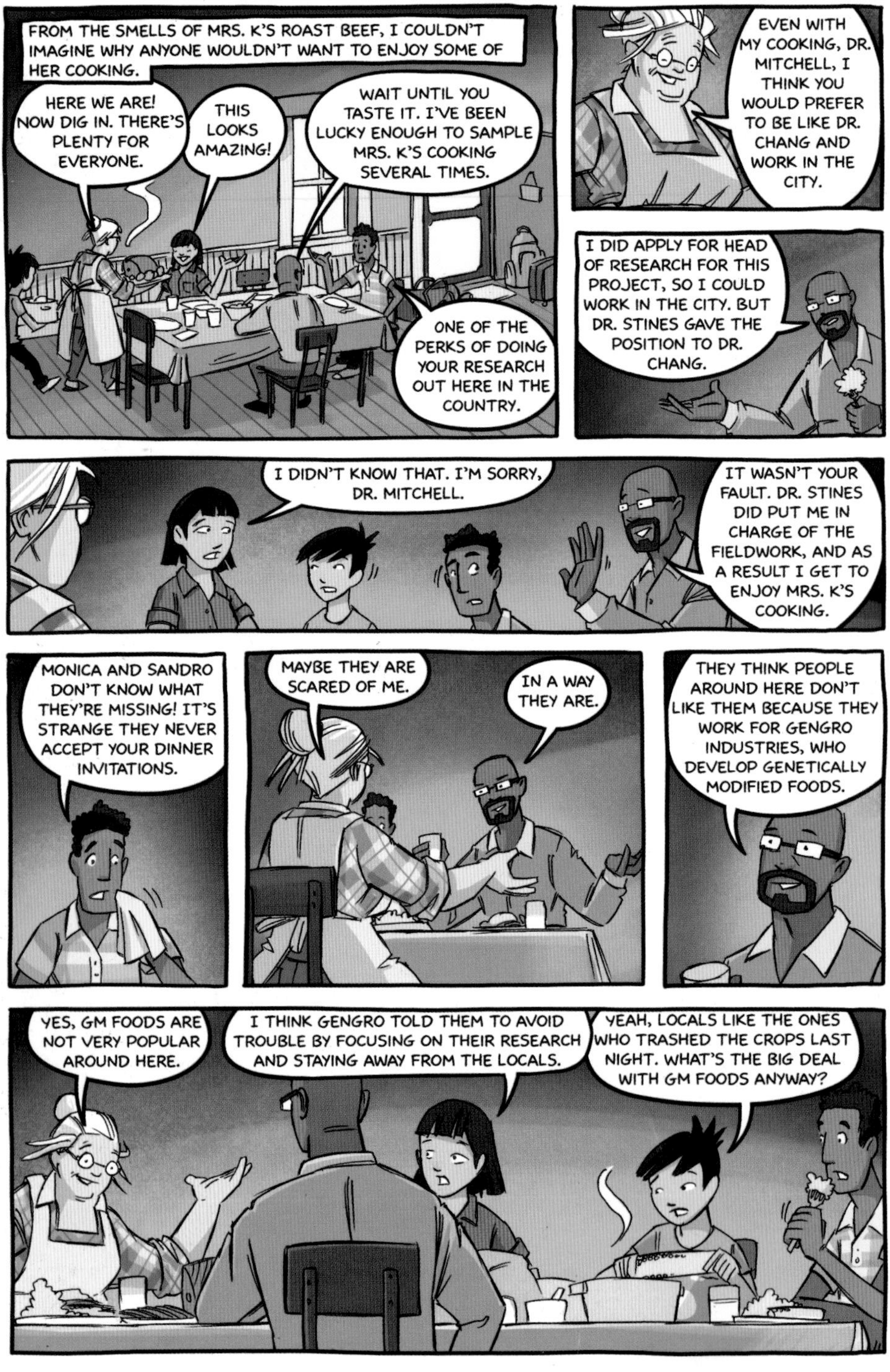
FROM THE SMELLS OF MRS. K'S ROAST BEEF, I COULDN'T IMAGINE WHY ANYONE WOULDN'T WANT TO ENJOY SOME OF HER COOKING.
HERE WE ARE! NOW DIG IN. THERE'S PLENTY FOR EVERYONE.
THIS LOOKS AMAZING!
WAIT UNTIL YOU TASTE IT. I'VE BEEN LUCKY ENOUGH TO SAMPLE MRS. K'S COOKING SEVERAL TIMES.
ONE OF THE PERKS OF DOING YOUR RESEARCH OUT HERE IN THE COUNTRY.
EVEN WITH MY COOKING, DR. MITCHELL, I THINK YOU WOULD PREFER TO BE LIKE DR. CHANG AND WORK IN THE CITY.
I DID APPLY FOR HEAD OF RESEARCH FOR THIS PROJECT, SO I COULD WORK IN THE CITY. BUT DR. STINES GAVE THE POSITION TO DR. CHANG.
I DIDN'T KNOW THAT. I'M SORRY, DR. MITCHELL.
IT WASN'T YOUR FAULT. DR. STINES DID PUT ME IN CHARGE OF THE FIELDWORK, AND AS A RESULT I GET TO ENJOY MRS. K'S COOKING.
MONICA AND SANDRO DON'T KNOW WHAT THEY'RE MISSING! IT'S STRANGE THEY NEVER ACCEPT YOUR DINNER INVITATIONS.
MAYBE THEY ARE SCARED OF ME.
IN A WAY THEY ARE.
THEY THINK PEOPLE AROUND HERE DON'T LIKE THEM BECAUSE THEY WORK FOR GENGRO INDUSTRIES, WHO DEVELOP GENETICALLY MODIFIED FOODS.
YES, GM FOODS ARE NOT VERY POPULAR AROUND HERE.
I THINK GENGRO TOLD THEM TO AVOID TROUBLE BY FOCUSING ON THEIR RESEARCH AND STAYING AWAY FROM THE LOCALS.
YEAH, LOCALS LIKE THE ONES WHO TRASHED THE CROPS LAST NIGHT. WHAT'S THE BIG DEAL WITH GM FOODS ANYWAY?

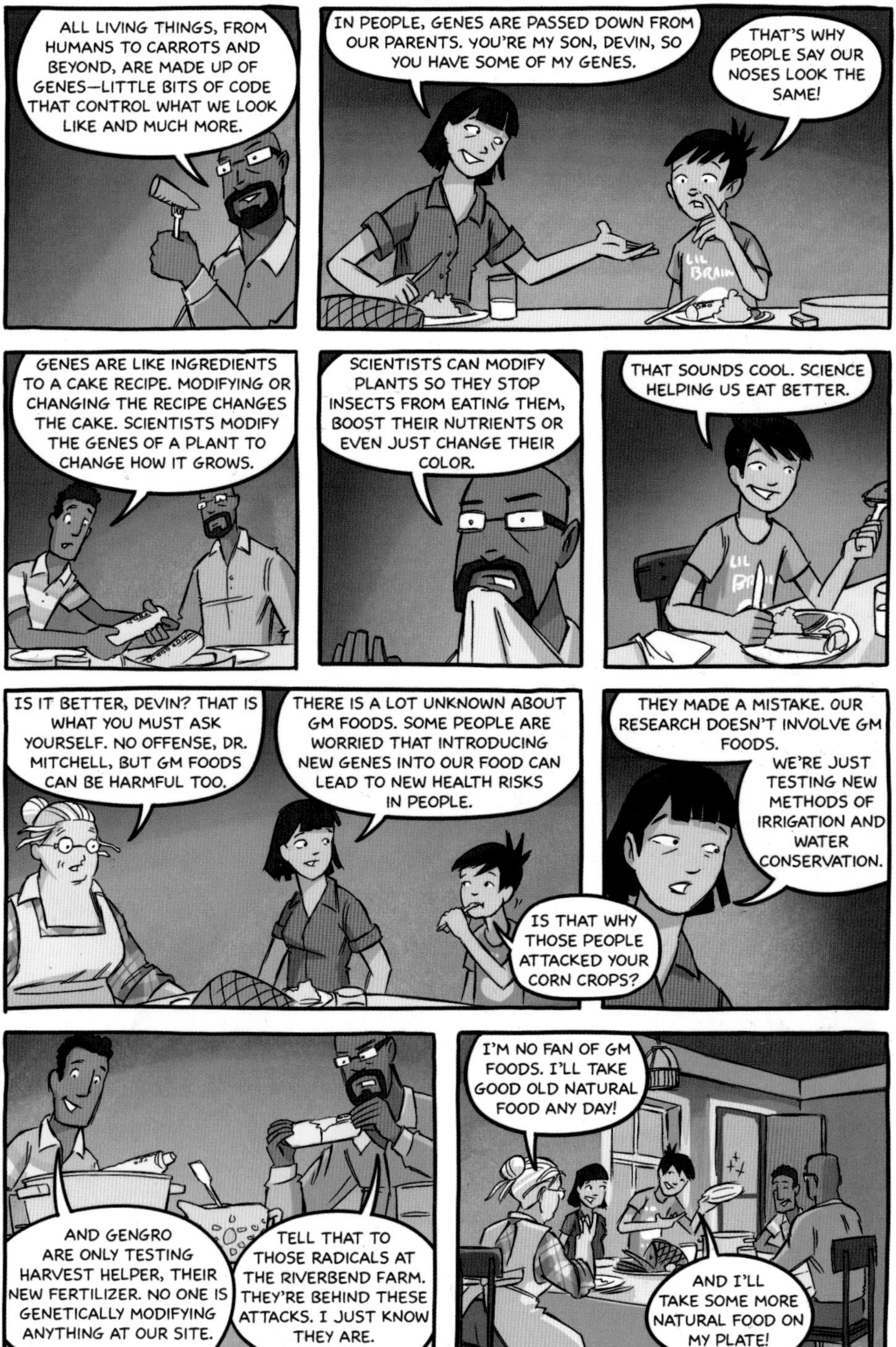
ALL LIVING THINGS, FROM HUMANS TO CARROTS AND BEYOND, ARE MADE UP OF GENES—LITTLE BITS OF CODE THAT CONTROL WHAT WE LOOK LIKE AND MUCH MORE.
IN PEOPLE, GENES ARE PASSED DOWN FROM OUR PARENTS. YOU'RE MY SON, DEVIN, SO YOU HAVE SOME OF MY GENES.
THAT'S WHY PEOPLE SAY OUR NOSES LOOK THE SAME!
LIL BRAIN
GENES ARE LIKE INGREDIENTS TO A CAKE RECIPE. MODIFYING OR CHANGING THE RECIPE CHANGES THE CAKE. SCIENTISTS MODIFY THE GENES OF A PLANT TO CHANGE HOW IT GROWS.
SCIENTISTS CAN MODIFY PLANTS SO THEY STOP INSECTS FROM EATING THEM, BOOST THEIR NUTRIENTS OR EVEN JUST CHANGE THEIR COLOR.
THAT SOUNDS COOL. SCIENCE HELPING US EAT BETTER.
IS IT BETTER, DEVIN? THAT IS WHAT YOU MUST ASK YOURSELF. NO OFFENSE, DR. MITCHELL, BUT GM FOODS CAN BE HARMFUL TOO.
THERE IS A LOT UNKNOWN ABOUT GM FOODS. SOME PEOPLE ARE WORRIED THAT INTRODUCING NEW GENES INTO OUR FOOD CAN LEAD TO NEW HEALTH RISKS IN PEOPLE.
IS THAT WHY THOSE PEOPLE ATTACKED YOUR CORN CROPS?
THEY MADE A MISTAKE. OUR RESEARCH DOESN'T INVOLVE GM FOODS.
WE'RE JUST TESTING NEW METHODS OF IRRIGATION AND WATER CONSERVATION.
AND GENGRO ARE ONLY TESTING HARVEST HELPER, THEIR NEW FERTILIZER. NO ONE IS GENETICALLY MODIFYING ANYTHING AT OUR SITE.
TELL THAT TO THOSE RADICALS AT THE RIVERBEND FARM. THEY'RE BEHIND THESE ATTACKS. I JUST KNOW THEY ARE.
I'M NO FAN OF GM FOODS. I'LL TAKE GOOD OLD NATURAL FOOD ANY DAY!
AND I'LL TAKE SOME MORE NATURAL FOOD ON MY PLATE!

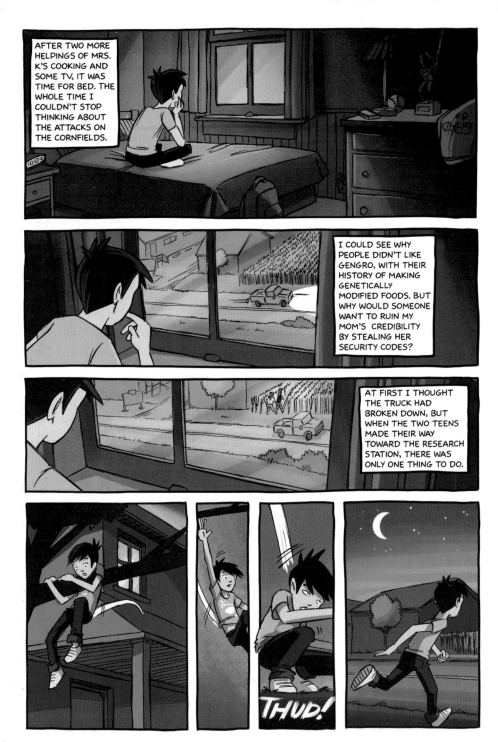

AFTER TWO MORE HELPINGS OF MRS. K'S COOKING AND SOME TV, IT WAS TIME FOR BED. THE WHOLE TIME I COULDN'T STOP THINKING ABOUT THE ATTACKS ON THE CORNFIELDS.

I COULD SEE WHY PEOPLE DIDN'T LIKE GENGRO, WITH THEIR HISTORY OF MAKING GENETICALLY MODIFIED FOODS. BUT WHY WOULD SOMEONE WANT TO RUIN MY MOM'S CREDIBILITY BY STEALING HER SECURITY CODES?

AT FIRST I THOUGHT THE TRUCK HAD BROKEN DOWN, BUT WHEN THE TWO TEENS MADE THEIR WAY TOWARD THE RESEARCH STATION, THERE WAS ONLY ONE THING TO DO.

THUD!

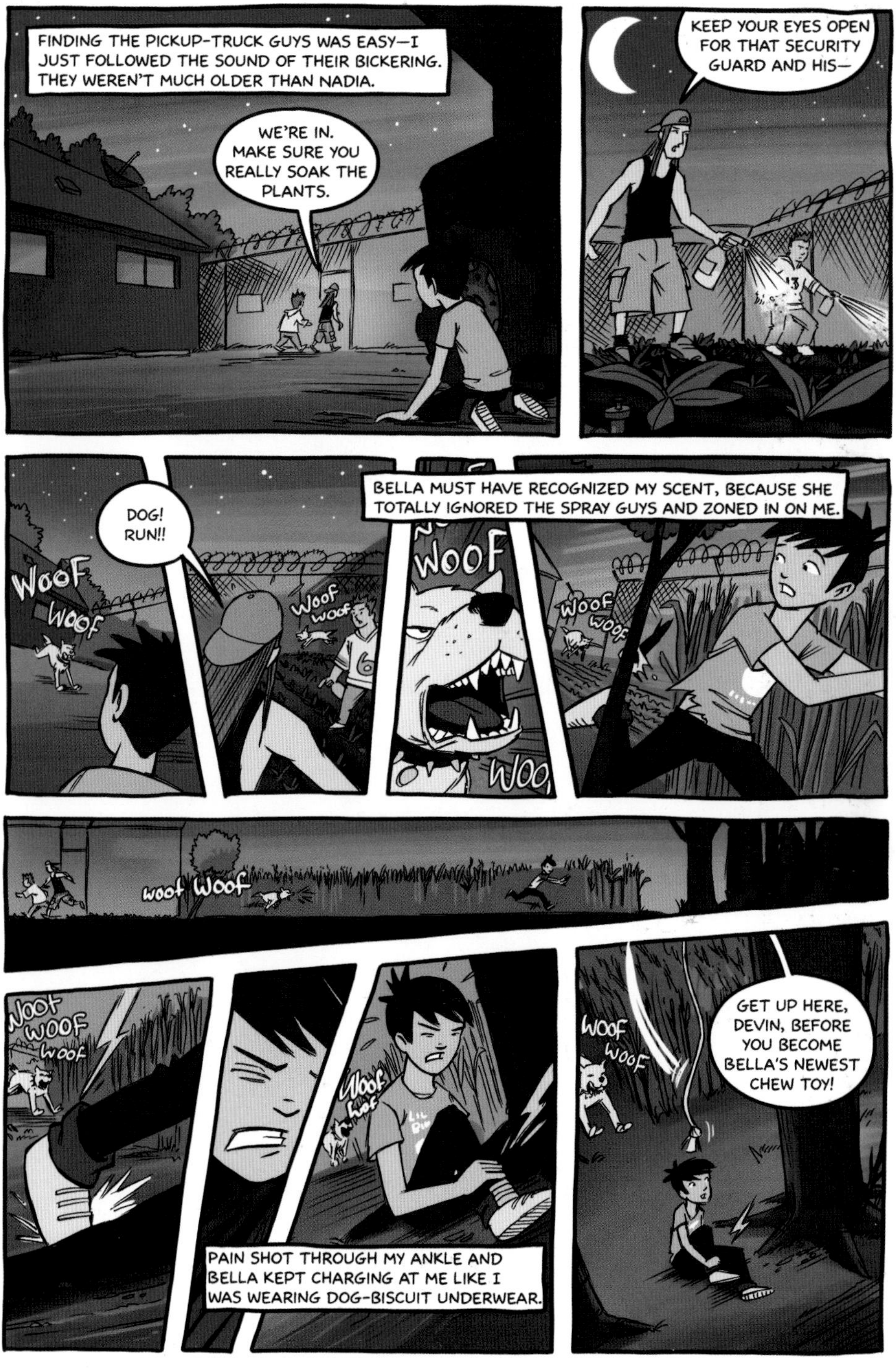
FINDING THE PICKUP-TRUCK GUYS WAS EASY—I JUST FOLLOWED THE SOUND OF THEIR BICKERING. THEY WEREN'T MUCH OLDER THAN NADIA.
WE'RE IN. MAKE SURE YOU REALLY SOAK THE PLANTS.
KEEP YOUR EYES OPEN FOR THAT SECURITY GUARD AND HIS—
DOG! RUN!!
WOOF
WOOF
WOOF
WOOF
BELLA MUST HAVE RECOGNIZED MY SCENT, BECAUSE SHE TOTALLY IGNORED THE SPRAY GUYS AND ZONED IN ON ME.
WOOF
WOOF
WOOF
WOOF
WOOF
WOOF
WOOF
WOOF
WOOF
WOOF
PAIN SHOT THROUGH MY ANKLE AND BELLA KEPT CHARGING AT ME LIKE I WAS WEARING DOG-BISCUIT UNDERWEAR.
WOOF
WOOF
GET UP HERE, DEVIN, BEFORE YOU BECOME BELLA'S NEWEST CHEW TOY!

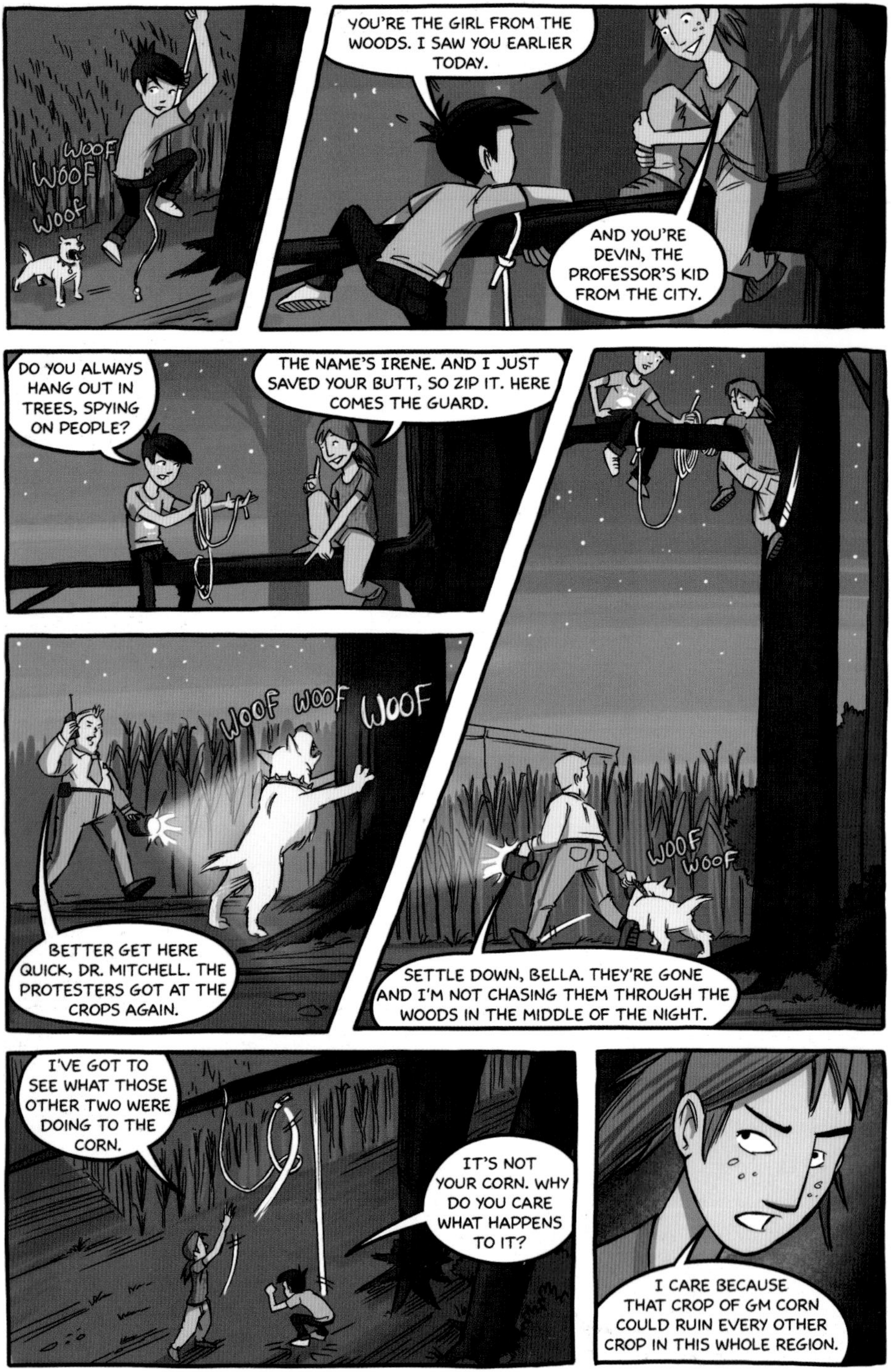
WOOF
WOOF
WOOF
YOU'RE THE GIRL FROM THE WOODS. I SAW YOU EARLIER TODAY.
AND YOU'RE DEVIN, THE PROFESSOR'S KID FROM THE CITY.
DO YOU ALWAYS HANG OUT IN TREES, SPYING ON PEOPLE?
THE NAME'S IRENE. AND I JUST SAVED YOUR BUTT, SO ZIP IT. HERE COMES THE GUARD.
WOOF WOOF WOOF
BETTER GET HERE QUICK, DR. MITCHELL. THE PROTESTERS GOT AT THE CROPS AGAIN.
WOOF
WOOF
SETTLE DOWN, BELLA. THEY'RE GONE AND I'M NOT CHASING THEM THROUGH THE WOODS IN THE MIDDLE OF THE NIGHT.
I'VE GOT TO SEE WHAT THOSE OTHER TWO WERE DOING TO THE CORN.
IT'S NOT YOUR CORN. WHY DO YOU CARE WHAT HAPPENS TO IT?
I CARE BECAUSE THAT CROP OF GM CORN COULD RUIN EVERY OTHER CROP IN THIS WHOLE REGION.

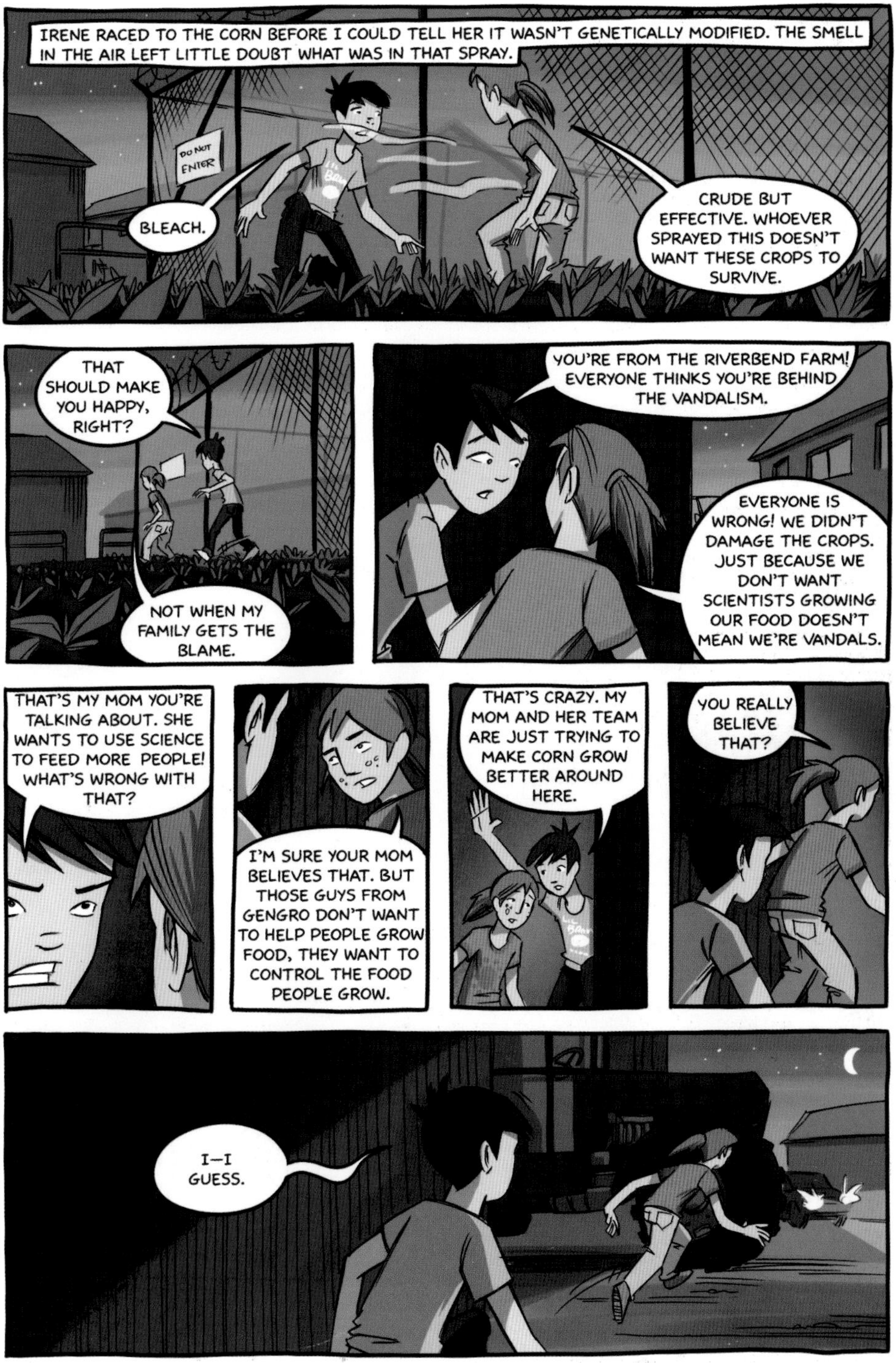
IRENE RACED TO THE CORN BEFORE I COULD TELL HER IT WASN'T GENETICALLY MODIFIED. THE SMELL IN THE AIR LEFT LITTLE DOUBT WHAT WAS IN THAT SPRAY.
DO NOT ENTER
BLEACH.
CRUDE BUT EFFECTIVE. WHOEVER SPRAYED THIS DOESN'T WANT THESE CROPS TO SURVIVE.
THAT SHOULD MAKE YOU HAPPY, RIGHT?
NOT WHEN MY FAMILY GETS THE BLAME.
YOU'RE FROM THE RIVERBEND FARM! EVERYONE THINKS YOU'RE BEHIND THE VANDALISM.
EVERYONE IS WRONG! WE DIDN'T DAMAGE THE CROPS. JUST BECAUSE WE DON'T WANT SCIENTISTS GROWING OUR FOOD DOESN'T MEAN WE'RE VANDALS.
THAT'S MY MOM YOU'RE TALKING ABOUT. SHE WANTS TO USE SCIENCE TO FEED MORE PEOPLE! WHAT'S WRONG WITH THAT?
I'M SURE YOUR MOM BELIEVES THAT. BUT THOSE GUYS FROM GENGRO DON'T WANT TO HELP PEOPLE GROW FOOD, THEY WANT TO CONTROL THE FOOD PEOPLE GROW.
THAT'S CRAZY. MY MOM AND HER TEAM ARE JUST TRYING TO MAKE CORN GROW BETTER AROUND HERE.
YOU REALLY BELIEVE THAT?
I—I GUESS.

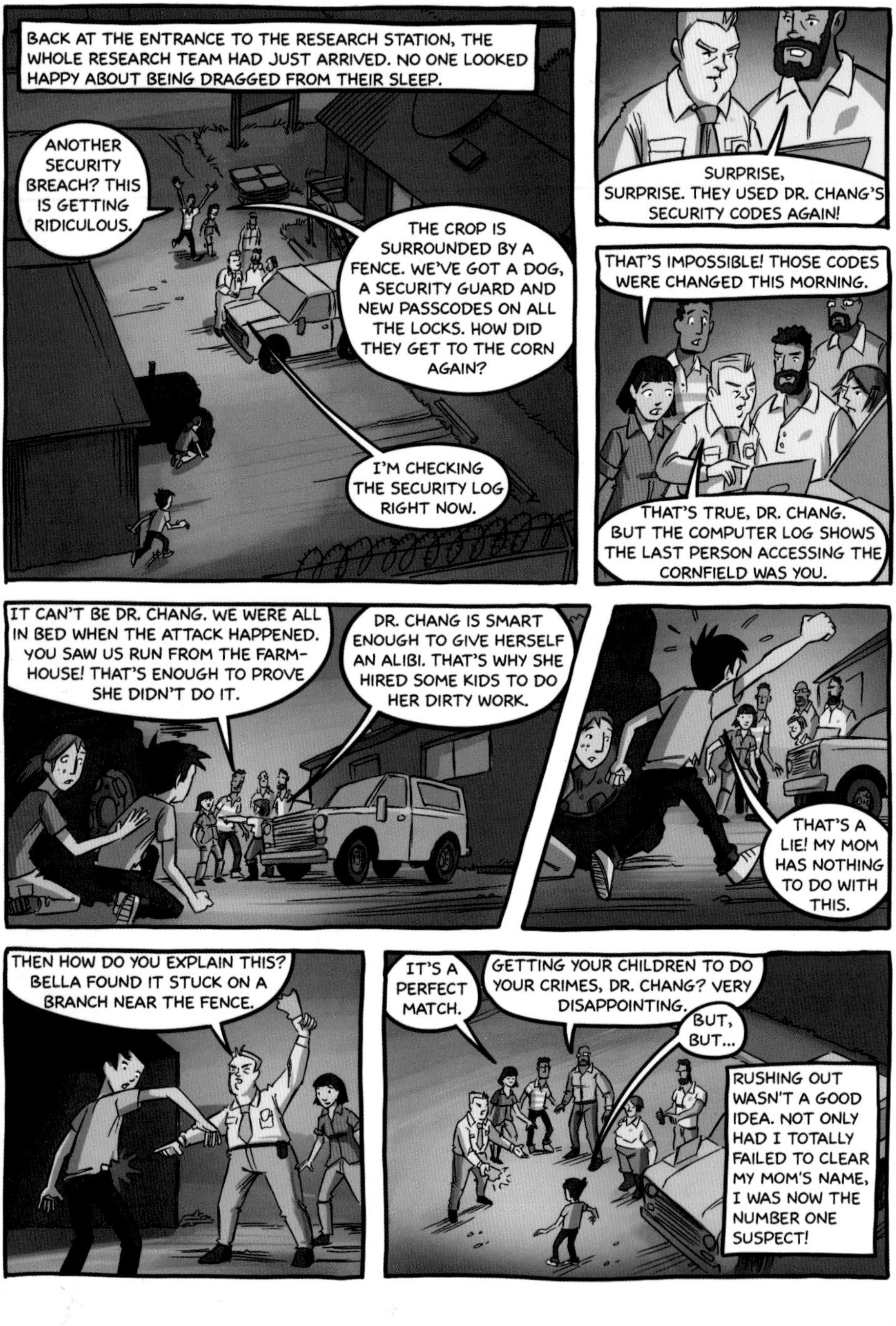
BACK AT THE ENTRANCE TO THE RESEARCH STATION, THE WHOLE RESEARCH TEAM HAD JUST ARRIVED. NO ONE LOOKED HAPPY ABOUT BEING DRAGGED FROM THEIR SLEEP.
ANOTHER SECURITY BREACH? THIS IS GETTING RIDICULOUS.
THE CROP IS SURROUNDED BY A FENCE. WE'VE GOT A DOG, A SECURITY GUARD AND NEW PASSCODES ON ALL THE LOCKS. HOW DID THEY GET TO THE CORN AGAIN?
I'M CHECKING THE SECURITY LOG RIGHT NOW.
SURPRISE, SURPRISE. THEY USED DR. CHANG'S SECURITY CODES AGAIN!
THAT'S IMPOSSIBLE! THOSE CODES WERE CHANGED THIS MORNING.
THAT'S TRUE, DR. CHANG. BUT THE COMPUTER LOG SHOWS THE LAST PERSON ACCESSING THE CORNFIELD WAS YOU.
IT CAN'T BE DR. CHANG. WE WERE ALL IN BED WHEN THE ATTACK HAPPENED. YOU SAW US RUN FROM THE FARM-HOUSE! THAT'S ENOUGH TO PROVE SHE DIDN'T DO IT.
DR. CHANG IS SMART ENOUGH TO GIVE HERSELF AN ALIBI. THAT'S WHY SHE HIRED SOME KIDS TO DO HER DIRTY WORK.
THAT'S A LIE! MY MOM HAS NOTHING TO DO WITH THIS.
THEN HOW DO YOU EXPLAIN THIS? BELLA FOUND IT STUCK ON A BRANCH NEAR THE FENCE.
IT'S A PERFECT MATCH.
GETTING YOUR CHILDREN TO DO YOUR CRIMES, DR. CHANG? VERY DISAPPOINTING.
BUT, BUT...
RUSHING OUT WASN'T A GOOD IDEA. NOT ONLY HAD I TOTALLY FAILED TO CLEAR MY MOM'S NAME, I WAS NOW THE NUMBER ONE SUSPECT!

CHAPTER 4
TO CATCH A CREEP

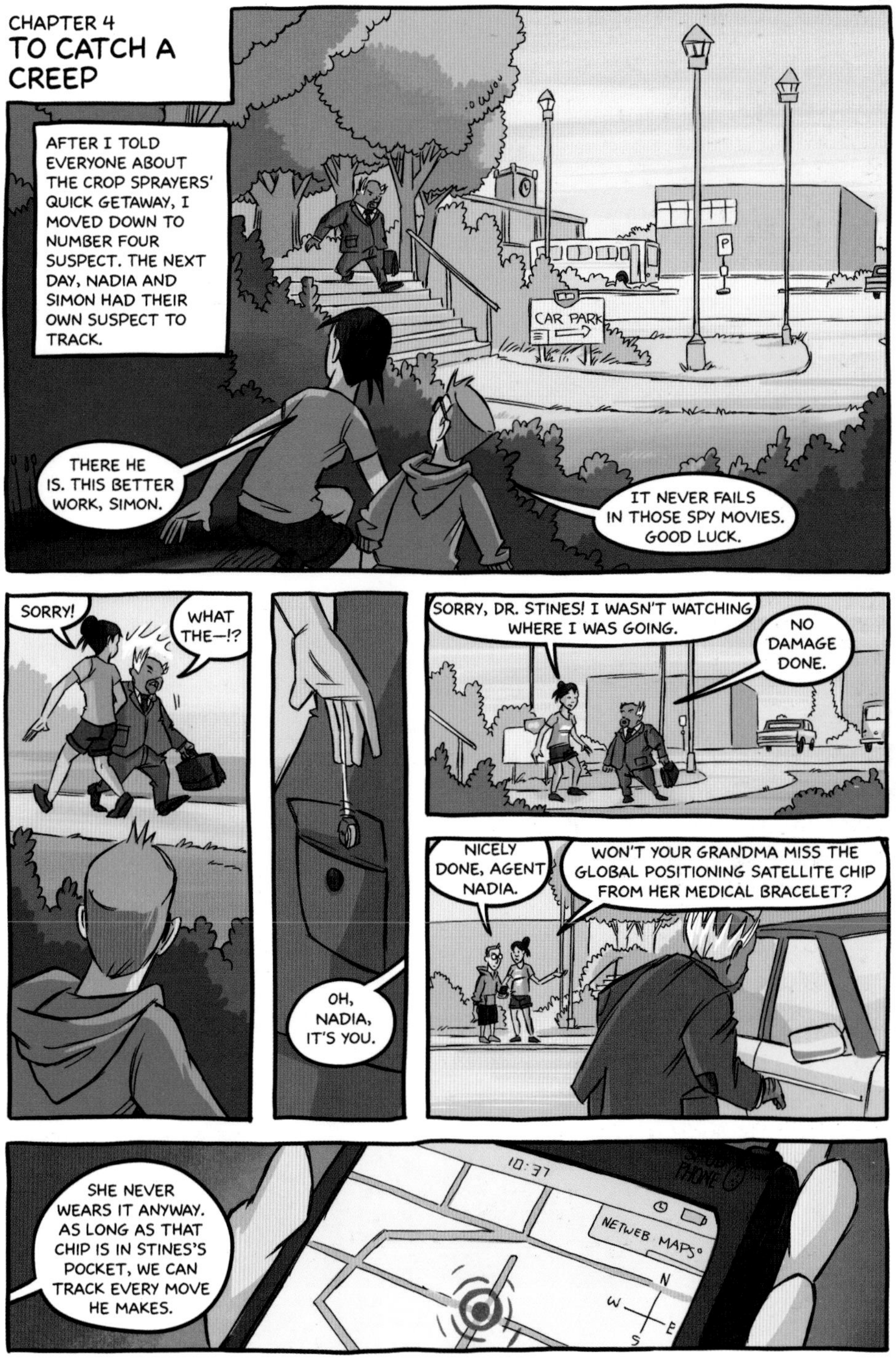

AFTER I TOLD EVERYONE ABOUT THE CROP SPRAYERS' QUICK GETAWAY, I MOVED DOWN TO NUMBER FOUR SUSPECT. THE NEXT DAY, NADIA AND SIMON HAD THEIR OWN SUSPECT TO TRACK.
CAR PARK
P
THERE HE IS. THIS BETTER WORK, SIMON.
IT NEVER FAILS IN THOSE SPY MOVIES. GOOD LUCK.
SORRY!
WHAT THE—!?
OH, NADIA, IT'S YOU.
SORRY, DR. STINES! I WASN'T WATCHING WHERE I WAS GOING.
NO DAMAGE DONE.
NICELY DONE, AGENT NADIA.
WON'T YOUR GRANDMA MISS THE GLOBAL POSITIONING SATELLITE CHIP FROM HER MEDICAL BRACELET?
SHE NEVER WEARS IT ANYWAY. AS LONG AS THAT CHIP IS IN STINES'S POCKET, WE CAN TRACK EVERY MOVE HE MAKES.
10:37
NETWEB MAPS
N
W
E
S

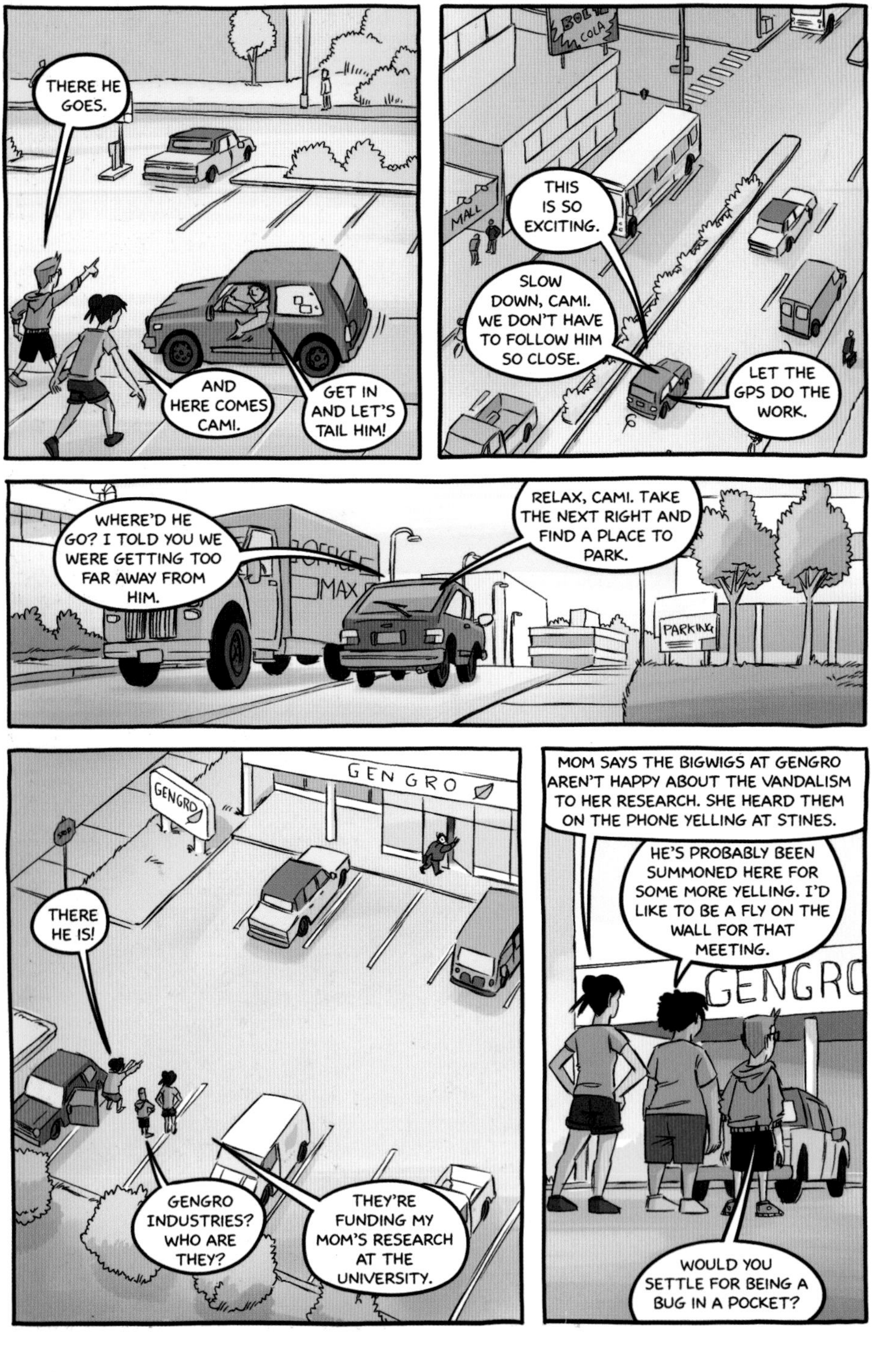

THERE HE GOES.
AND HERE COMES CAMI.
GET IN AND LET'S TAIL HIM!
BOLT COLA
MALL
THIS IS SO EXCITING.
SLOW DOWN, CAMI. WE DON'T HAVE TO FOLLOW HIM SO CLOSE.
LET THE GPS DO THE WORK.
WHERE'D HE GO? I TOLD YOU WE WERE GETTING TOO FAR AWAY FROM HIM.
RELAX, CAMI. TAKE THE NEXT RIGHT AND FIND A PLACE TO PARK.
OFFICE MAX
PARKING
GENGRO
GENGRO
THERE HE IS!
GENGRO INDUSTRIES? WHO ARE THEY?
THEY'RE FUNDING MY MOM'S RESEARCH AT THE UNIVERSITY.
MOM SAYS THE BIGWIGS AT GENGRO AREN'T HAPPY ABOUT THE VANDALISM TO HER RESEARCH. SHE HEARD THEM ON THE PHONE YELLING AT STINES.
HE'S PROBABLY BEEN SUMMONED HERE FOR SOME MORE YELLING. I'D LIKE TO BE A FLY ON THE WALL FOR THAT MEETING.
GENGRO
WOULD YOU SETTLE FOR BEING A BUG IN A POCKET?

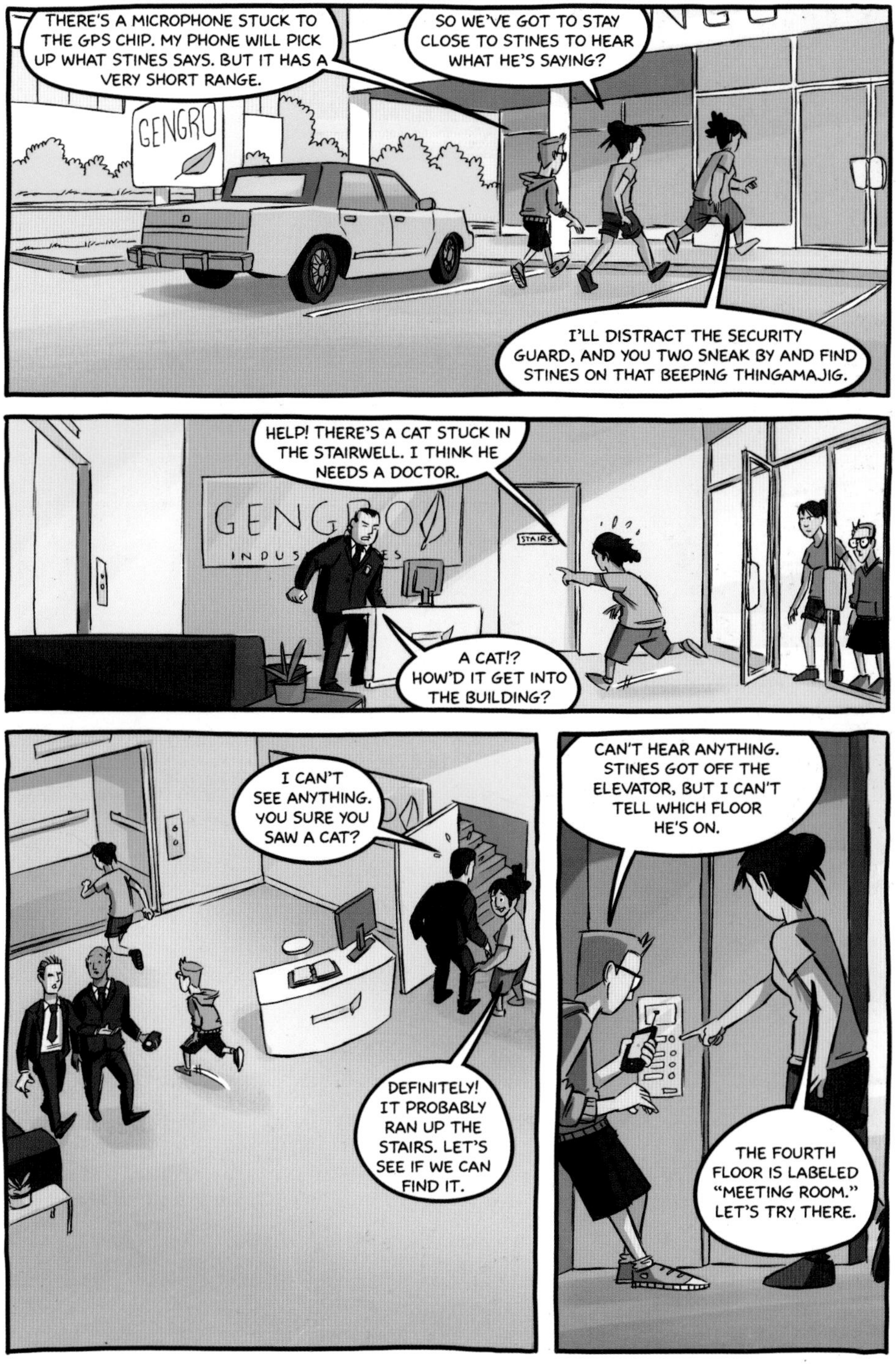
THERE'S A MICROPHONE STUCK TO THE GPS CHIP. MY PHONE WILL PICK UP WHAT STINES SAYS. BUT IT HAS A VERY SHORT RANGE.
SO WE'VE GOT TO STAY CLOSE TO STINES TO HEAR WHAT HE'S SAYING?
GENGRO
I'LL DISTRACT THE SECURITY GUARD, AND YOU TWO SNEAK BY AND FIND STINES ON THAT BEEPING THINGAMAJIG.
HELP! THERE'S A CAT STUCK IN THE STAIRWELL. I THINK HE NEEDS A DOCTOR.
STAIRS
A CAT!? HOW'D IT GET INTO THE BUILDING?
I CAN'T SEE ANYTHING. YOU SURE YOU SAW A CAT?
DEFINITELY! IT PROBABLY RAN UP THE STAIRS. LET'S SEE IF WE CAN FIND IT.
CAN'T HEAR ANYTHING. STINES GOT OFF THE ELEVATOR, BUT I CAN'T TELL WHICH FLOOR HE'S ON.
THE FOURTH FLOOR IS LABELED "MEETING ROOM." LET'S TRY THERE.

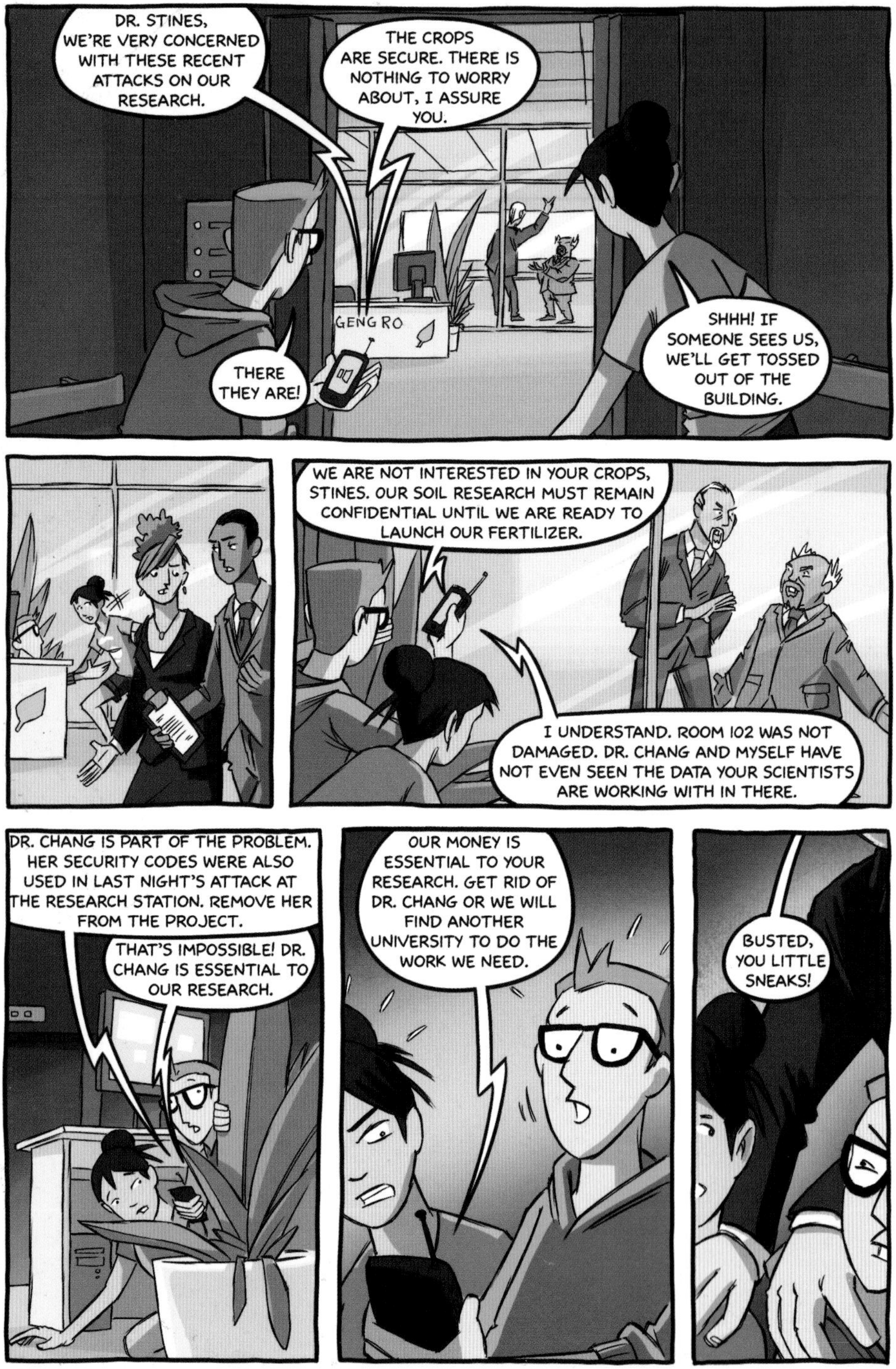
DR. STINES, WE'RE VERY CONCERNED WITH THESE RECENT ATTACKS ON OUR RESEARCH.
THE CROPS ARE SECURE. THERE IS NOTHING TO WORRY ABOUT, I ASSURE YOU.
GENGRO
THERE THEY ARE!
SHHH! IF SOMEONE SEES US, WE'LL GET TOSSED OUT OF THE BUILDING.
WE ARE NOT INTERESTED IN YOUR CROPS, STINES. OUR SOIL RESEARCH MUST REMAIN CONFIDENTIAL UNTIL WE ARE READY TO LAUNCH OUR FERTILIZER.
I UNDERSTAND. ROOM 102 WAS NOT DAMAGED. DR. CHANG AND MYSELF HAVE NOT EVEN SEEN THE DATA YOUR SCIENTISTS ARE WORKING WITH IN THERE.
DR. CHANG IS PART OF THE PROBLEM. HER SECURITY CODES WERE ALSO USED IN LAST NIGHT'S ATTACK AT THE RESEARCH STATION. REMOVE HER FROM THE PROJECT.
THAT'S IMPOSSIBLE! DR. CHANG IS ESSENTIAL TO OUR RESEARCH.
OUR MONEY IS ESSENTIAL TO YOUR RESEARCH. GET RID OF DR. CHANG OR WE WILL FIND ANOTHER UNIVERSITY TO DO THE WORK WE NEED.
BUSTED, YOU LITTLE SNEAKS!

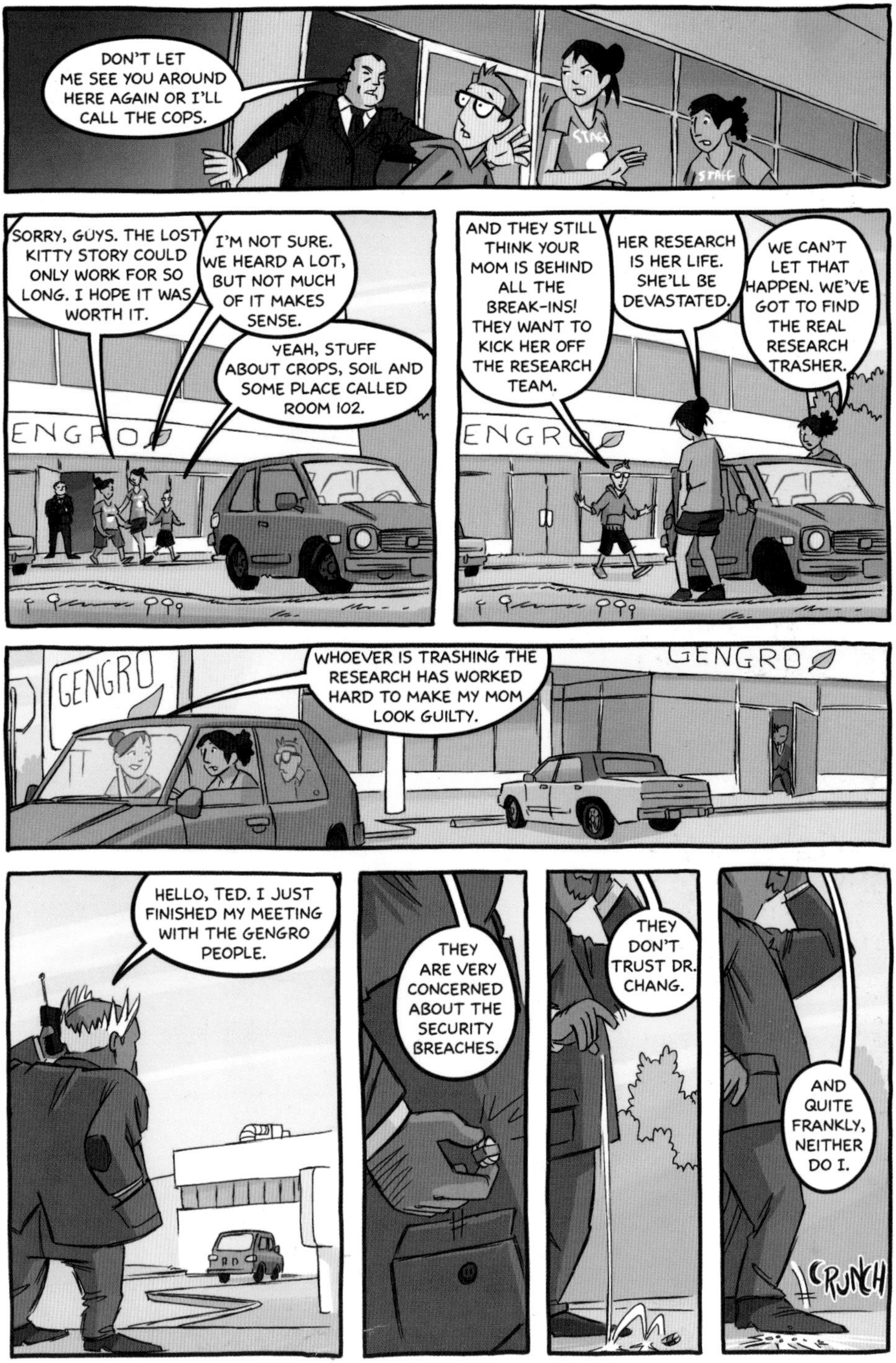
DON'T LET ME SEE YOU AROUND HERE AGAIN OR I'LL CALL THE COPS.
STAFF
STAFF
SORRY, GUYS. THE LOST KITTY STORY COULD ONLY WORK FOR SO LONG. I HOPE IT WAS WORTH IT.
I'M NOT SURE. WE HEARD A LOT, BUT NOT MUCH OF IT MAKES SENSE.
YEAH, STUFF ABOUT CROPS, SOIL AND SOME PLACE CALLED ROOM 102.
ENGRO
AND THEY STILL THINK YOUR MOM IS BEHIND ALL THE BREAK-INS! THEY WANT TO KICK HER OFF THE RESEARCH TEAM.
HER RESEARCH IS HER LIFE. SHE'LL BE DEVASTATED.
WE CAN'T LET THAT HAPPEN. WE'VE GOT TO FIND THE REAL RESEARCH TRASHER.
ENGRO
GENGRO
WHOEVER IS TRASHING THE RESEARCH HAS WORKED HARD TO MAKE MY MOM LOOK GUILTY.
GENGRO
HELLO, TED. I JUST FINISHED MY MEETING WITH THE GENGRO PEOPLE.
THEY ARE VERY CONCERNED ABOUT THE SECURITY BREACHES.
THEY DON'T TRUST DR. CHANG.
AND QUITE FRANKLY, NEITHER DO I.
CRUNCH

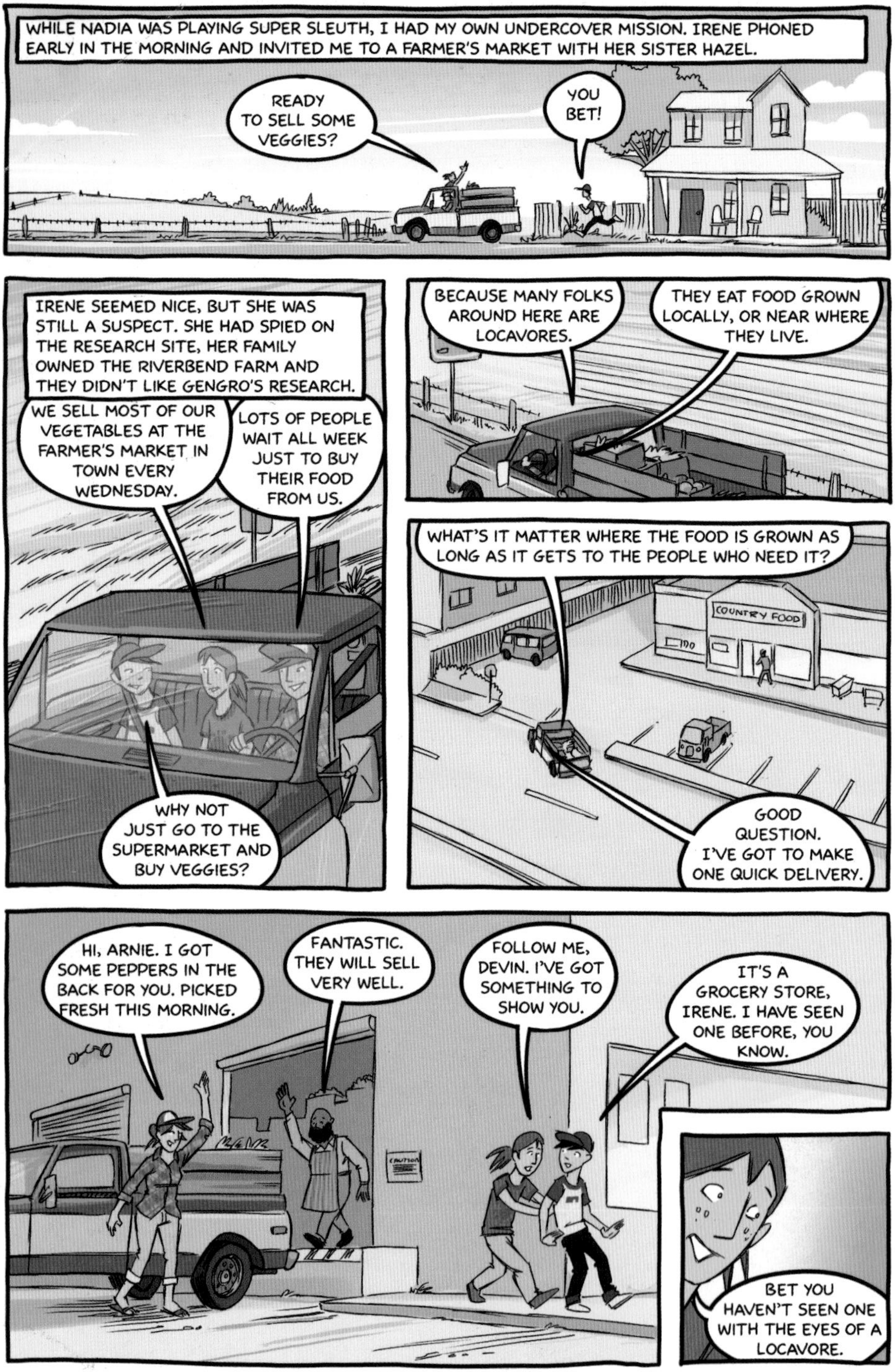
WHILE NADIA WAS PLAYING SUPER SLEUTH, I HAD MY OWN UNDERCOVER MISSION. IRENE PHONED EARLY IN THE MORNING AND INVITED ME TO A FARMER'S MARKET WITH HER SISTER HAZEL.
READY TO SELL SOME VEGGIES?
YOU BET!
IRENE SEEMED NICE, BUT SHE WAS STILL A SUSPECT. SHE HAD SPIED ON THE RESEARCH SITE, HER FAMILY OWNED THE RIVERBEND FARM AND THEY DIDN'T LIKE GENGRO'S RESEARCH.
WE SELL MOST OF OUR VEGETABLES AT THE FARMER'S MARKET IN TOWN EVERY WEDNESDAY.
LOTS OF PEOPLE WAIT ALL WEEK JUST TO BUY THEIR FOOD FROM US.
WHY NOT JUST GO TO THE SUPERMARKET AND BUY VEGGIES?
BECAUSE MANY FOLKS AROUND HERE ARE LOCAVORES.
THEY EAT FOOD GROWN LOCALLY, OR NEAR WHERE THEY LIVE.
WHAT'S IT MATTER WHERE THE FOOD IS GROWN AS LONG AS IT GETS TO THE PEOPLE WHO NEED IT?
COUNTRY FOOD
GOOD QUESTION. I'VE GOT TO MAKE ONE QUICK DELIVERY.
HI, ARNIE. I GOT SOME PEPPERS IN THE BACK FOR YOU. PICKED FRESH THIS MORNING.
FANTASTIC. THEY WILL SELL VERY WELL.
FOLLOW ME, DEVIN. I'VE GOT SOMETHING TO SHOW YOU.
IT'S A GROCERY STORE, IRENE. I HAVE SEEN ONE BEFORE, YOU KNOW.
BET YOU HAVEN'T SEEN ONE WITH THE EYES OF A LOCAVORE.

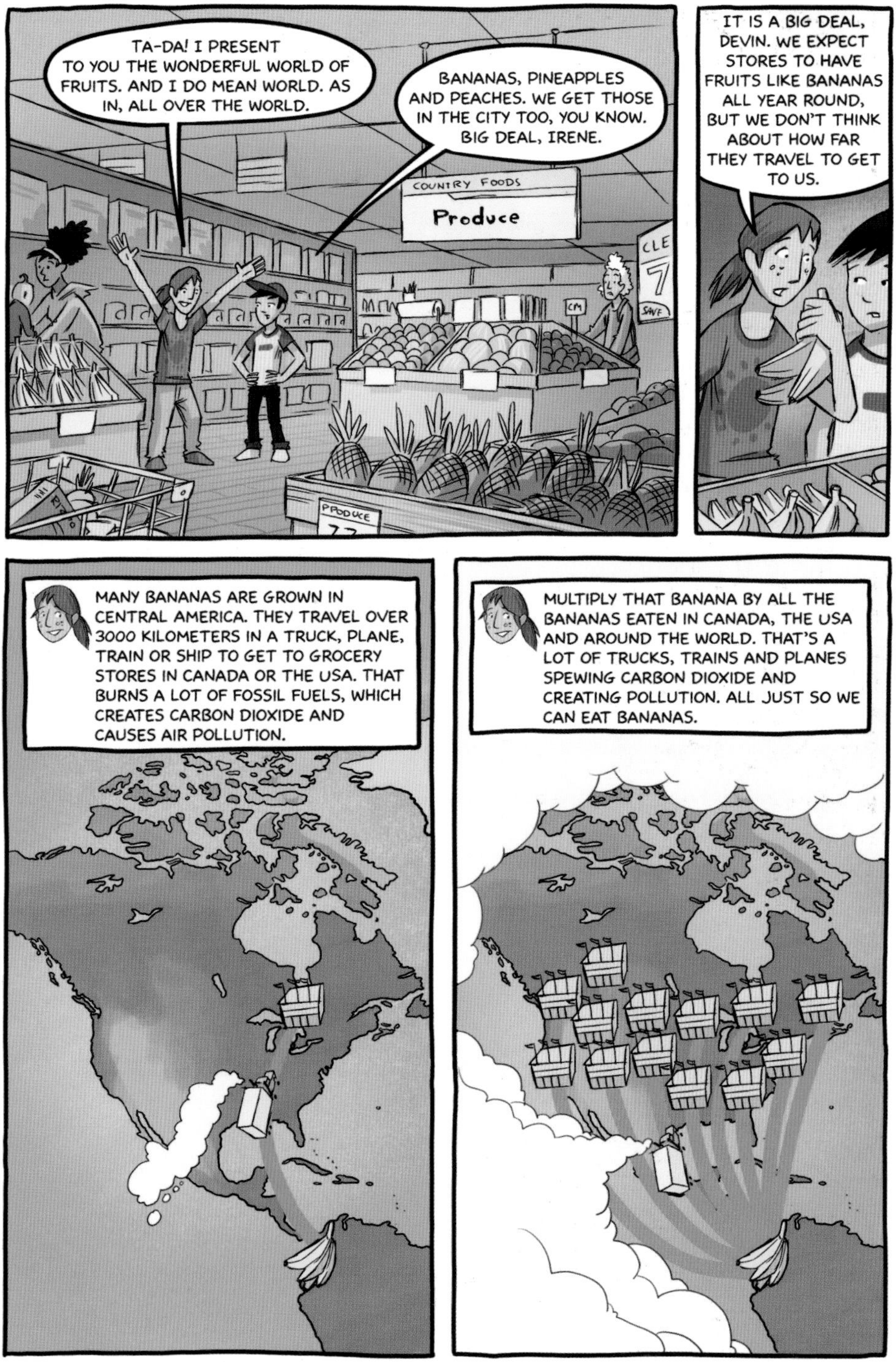
TA-DA! I PRESENT TO YOU THE WONDERFUL WORLD OF FRUITS. AND I DO MEAN WORLD. AS IN, ALL OVER THE WORLD.
BANANAS, PINEAPPLES AND PEACHES. WE GET THOSE IN THE CITY TOO, YOU KNOW. BIG DEAL, IRENE.
COUNTRY FOODS
Produce
IT IS A BIG DEAL, DEVIN. WE EXPECT STORES TO HAVE FRUITS LIKE BANANAS ALL YEAR ROUND, BUT WE DON'T THINK ABOUT HOW FAR THEY TRAVEL TO GET TO US.
MANY BANANAS ARE GROWN IN CENTRAL AMERICA. THEY TRAVEL OVER 3000 KILOMETERS IN A TRUCK, PLANE, TRAIN OR SHIP TO GET TO GROCERY STORES IN CANADA OR THE USA. THAT BURNS A LOT OF FOSSIL FUELS, WHICH CREATES CARBON DIOXIDE AND CAUSES AIR POLLUTION.
MULTIPLY THAT BANANA BY ALL THE BANANAS EATEN IN CANADA, THE USA AND AROUND THE WORLD. THAT'S A LOT OF TRUCKS, TRAINS AND PLANES SPEWING CARBON DIOXIDE AND CREATING POLLUTION. ALL JUST SO WE CAN EAT BANANAS.

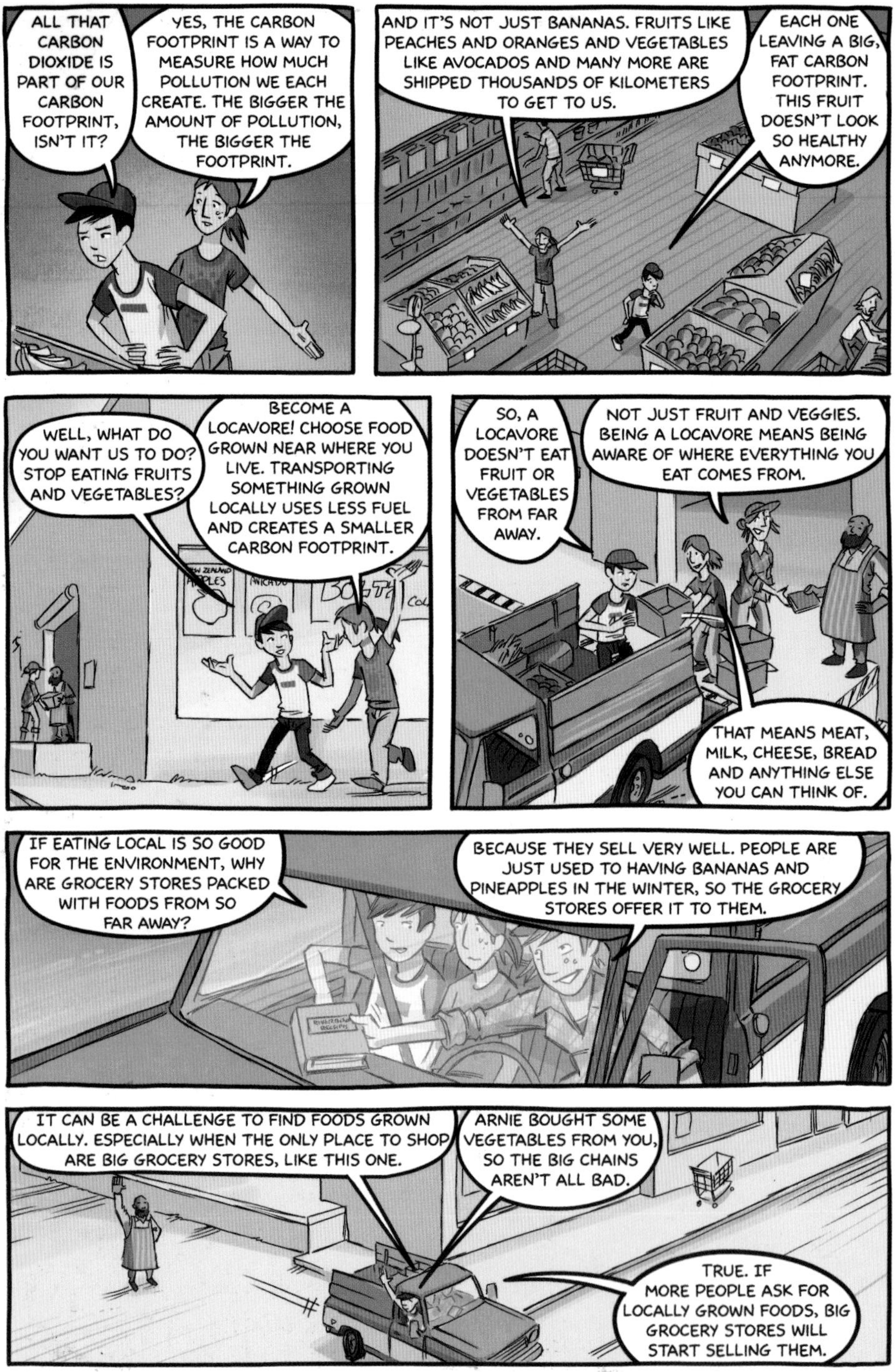
ALL THAT CARBON DIOXIDE IS PART OF OUR CARBON FOOTPRINT, ISN'T IT?
YES, THE CARBON FOOTPRINT IS A WAY TO MEASURE HOW MUCH POLLUTION WE EACH CREATE. THE BIGGER THE AMOUNT OF POLLUTION, THE BIGGER THE FOOTPRINT.
AND IT'S NOT JUST BANANAS. FRUITS LIKE PEACHES AND ORANGES AND VEGETABLES LIKE AVOCADOS AND MANY MORE ARE SHIPPED THOUSANDS OF KILOMETERS TO GET TO US.
EACH ONE LEAVING A BIG, FAT CARBON FOOTPRINT. THIS FRUIT DOESN'T LOOK SO HEALTHY ANYMORE.
WELL, WHAT DO YOU WANT US TO DO? STOP EATING FRUITS AND VEGETABLES?
BECOME A LOCAVORE! CHOOSE FOOD GROWN NEAR WHERE YOU LIVE. TRANSPORTING SOMETHING GROWN LOCALLY USES LESS FUEL AND CREATES A SMALLER CARBON FOOTPRINT.
SO, A LOCAVORE DOESN'T EAT FRUIT OR VEGETABLES FROM FAR AWAY.
NOT JUST FRUIT AND VEGGIES. BEING A LOCAVORE MEANS BEING AWARE OF WHERE EVERYTHING YOU EAT COMES FROM.
THAT MEANS MEAT, MILK, CHEESE, BREAD AND ANYTHING ELSE YOU CAN THINK OF.
IF EATING LOCAL IS SO GOOD FOR THE ENVIRONMENT, WHY ARE GROCERY STORES PACKED WITH FOODS FROM SO FAR AWAY?
BECAUSE THEY SELL VERY WELL. PEOPLE ARE JUST USED TO HAVING BANANAS AND PINEAPPLES IN THE WINTER, SO THE GROCERY STORES OFFER IT TO THEM.
IT CAN BE A CHALLENGE TO FIND FOODS GROWN LOCALLY. ESPECIALLY WHEN THE ONLY PLACE TO SHOP ARE BIG GROCERY STORES, LIKE THIS ONE.
ARNIE BOUGHT SOME VEGETABLES FROM YOU, SO THE BIG CHAINS AREN'T ALL BAD.
TRUE. IF MORE PEOPLE ASK FOR LOCALLY GROWN FOODS, BIG GROCERY STORES WILL START SELLING THEM.

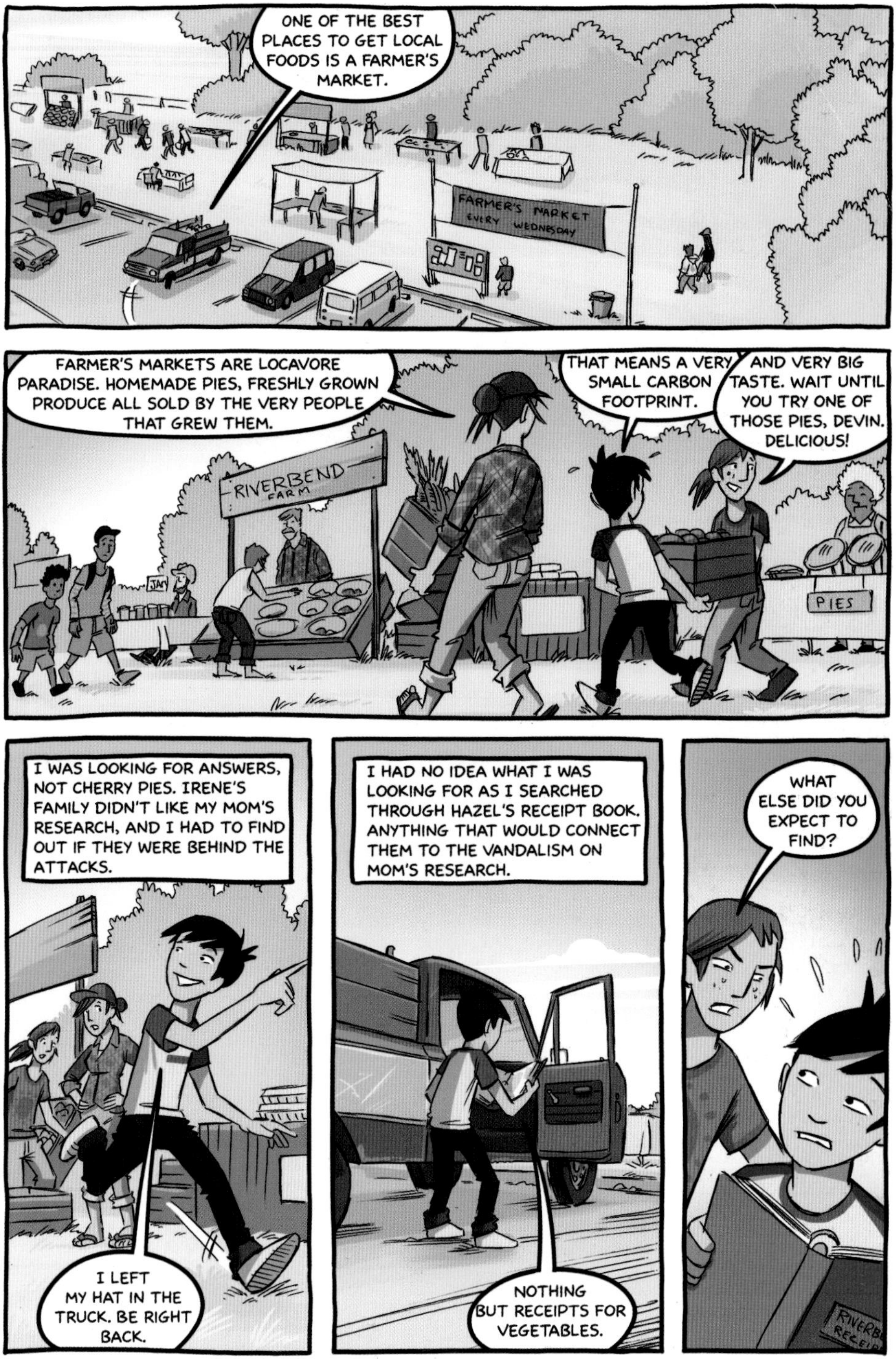
ONE OF THE BEST PLACES TO GET LOCAL FOODS IS A FARMER'S MARKET.
FARMER'S MARKET EVERY WEDNESDAY
FARMER'S MARKETS ARE LOCAVORE PARADISE. HOMEMADE PIES, FRESHLY GROWN PRODUCE ALL SOLD BY THE VERY PEOPLE THAT GREW THEM.
THAT MEANS A VERY SMALL CARBON FOOTPRINT.
AND VERY BIG TASTE. WAIT UNTIL YOU TRY ONE OF THOSE PIES, DEVIN. DELICIOUS!
RIVERBEND FARM
JAM
PIES
I WAS LOOKING FOR ANSWERS, NOT CHERRY PIES. IRENE'S FAMILY DIDN'T LIKE MY MOM'S RESEARCH, AND I HAD TO FIND OUT IF THEY WERE BEHIND THE ATTACKS.
I LEFT MY HAT IN THE TRUCK. BE RIGHT BACK.
I HAD NO IDEA WHAT I WAS LOOKING FOR AS I SEARCHED THROUGH HAZEL'S RECEIPT BOOK. ANYTHING THAT WOULD CONNECT THEM TO THE VANDALISM ON MOM'S RESEARCH.
NOTHING BUT RECEIPTS FOR VEGETABLES.
WHAT ELSE DID YOU EXPECT TO FIND?

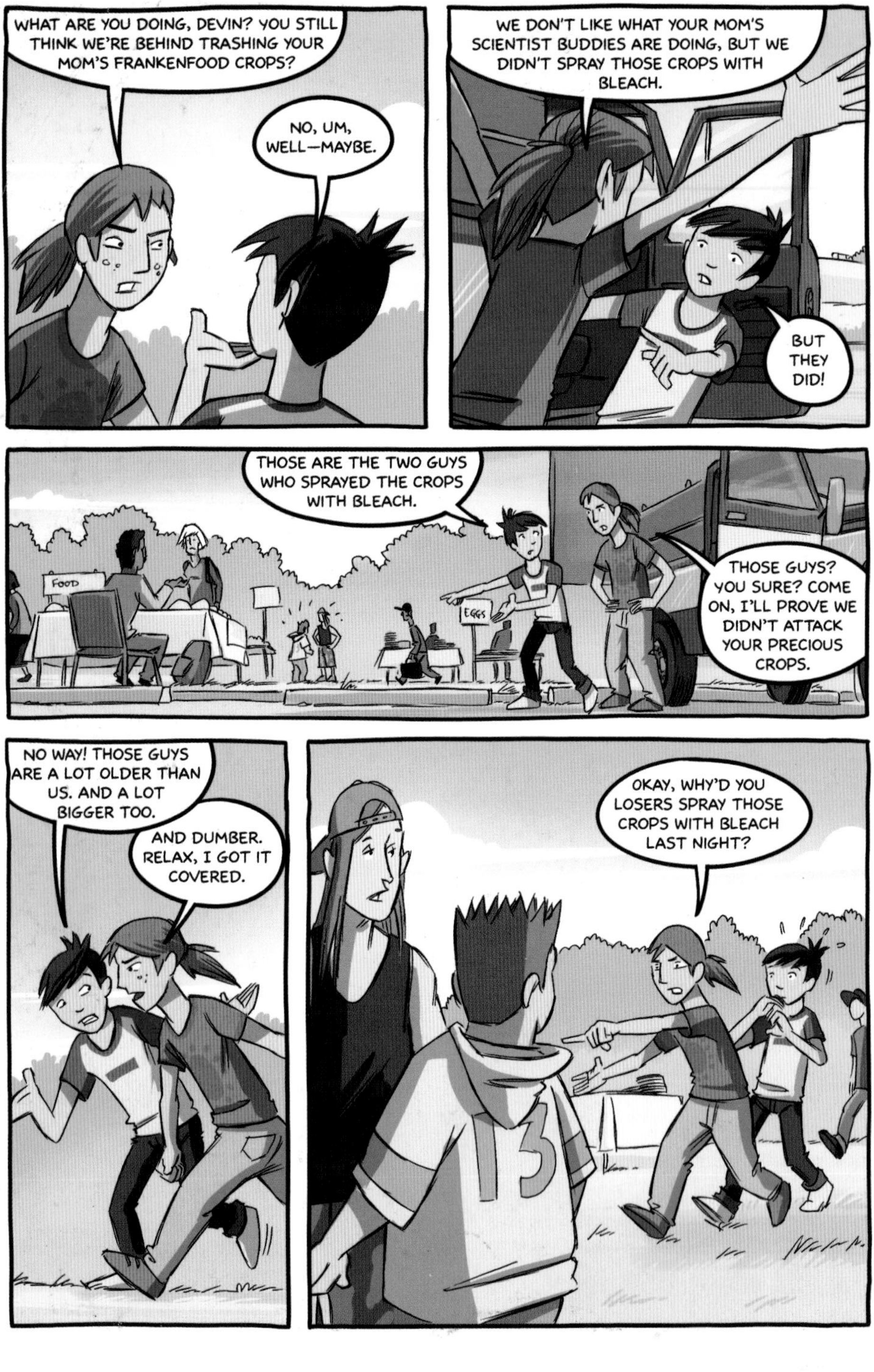
WHAT ARE YOU DOING, DEVIN? YOU STILL THINK WE'RE BEHIND TRASHING YOUR MOM'S FRANKENFOOD CROPS?
NO, UM, WELL—MAYBE.
WE DON'T LIKE WHAT YOUR MOM'S SCIENTIST BUDDIES ARE DOING, BUT WE DIDN'T SPRAY THOSE CROPS WITH BLEACH.
BUT THEY DID!
THOSE ARE THE TWO GUYS WHO SPRAYED THE CROPS WITH BLEACH.
FOOD
EGGS
THOSE GUYS? YOU SURE? COME ON, I'LL PROVE WE DIDN'T ATTACK YOUR PRECIOUS CROPS.
NO WAY! THOSE GUYS ARE A LOT OLDER THAN US. AND A LOT BIGGER TOO.
AND DUMBER. RELAX, I GOT IT COVERED.
OKAY, WHY'D YOU LOSERS SPRAY THOSE CROPS WITH BLEACH LAST NIGHT?
13

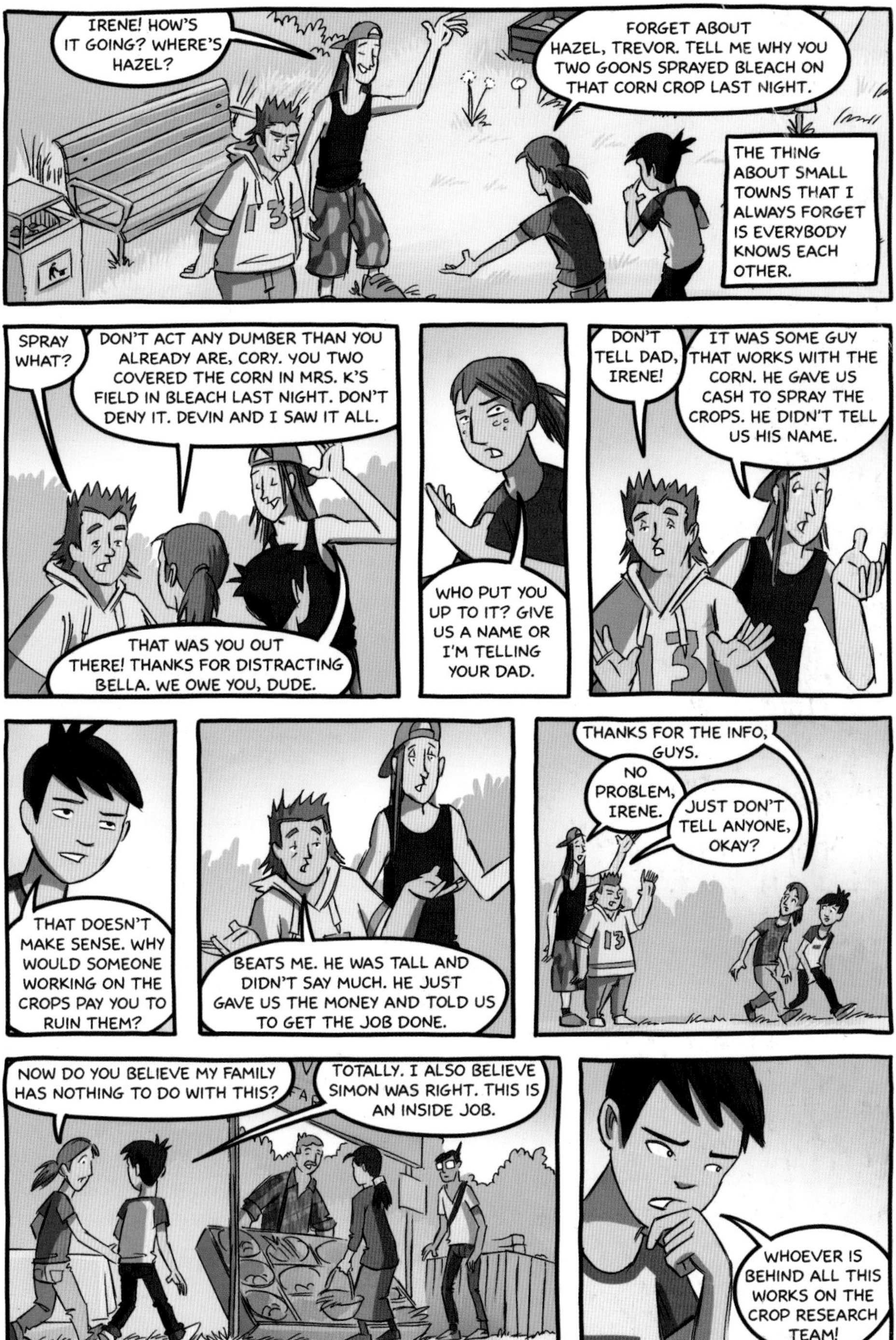

IRENE! HOW'S IT GOING? WHERE'S HAZEL?
FORGET ABOUT HAZEL, TREVOR. TELL ME WHY YOU TWO GOONS SPRAYED BLEACH ON THAT CORN CROP LAST NIGHT.
THE THING ABOUT SMALL TOWNS THAT I ALWAYS FORGET IS EVERYBODY KNOWS EACH OTHER.
SPRAY WHAT?
DON'T ACT ANY DUMBER THAN YOU ALREADY ARE, CORY. YOU TWO COVERED THE CORN IN MRS. K'S FIELD IN BLEACH LAST NIGHT. DON'T DENY IT. DEVIN AND I SAW IT ALL.
THAT WAS YOU OUT THERE! THANKS FOR DISTRACTING BELLA. WE OWE YOU, DUDE.
WHO PUT YOU UP TO IT? GIVE US A NAME OR I'M TELLING YOUR DAD.
DON'T TELL DAD, IRENE!
IT WAS SOME GUY THAT WORKS WITH THE CORN. HE GAVE US CASH TO SPRAY THE CROPS. HE DIDN'T TELL US HIS NAME.
THAT DOESN'T MAKE SENSE. WHY WOULD SOMEONE WORKING ON THE CROPS PAY YOU TO RUIN THEM?
BEATS ME. HE WAS TALL AND DIDN'T SAY MUCH. HE JUST GAVE US THE MONEY AND TOLD US TO GET THE JOB DONE.
THANKS FOR THE INFO, GUYS.
NO PROBLEM, IRENE.
JUST DON'T TELL ANYONE, OKAY?
NOW DO YOU BELIEVE MY FAMILY HAS NOTHING TO DO WITH THIS?
TOTALLY. I ALSO BELIEVE SIMON WAS RIGHT. THIS IS AN INSIDE JOB.
WHOEVER IS BEHIND ALL THIS WORKS ON THE CROP RESEARCH TEAM!

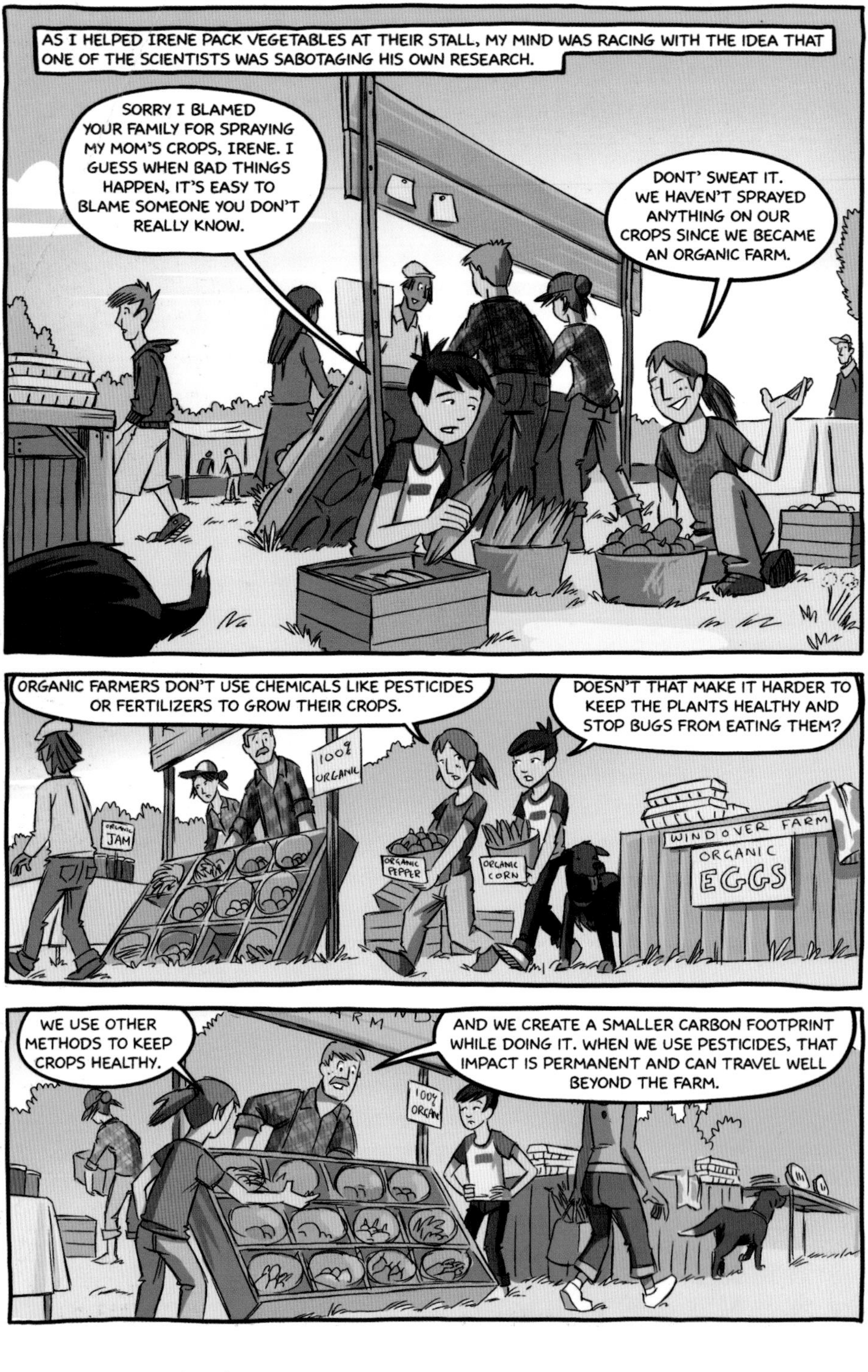
AS I HELPED IRENE PACK VEGETABLES AT THEIR STALL, MY MIND WAS RACING WITH THE IDEA THAT ONE OF THE SCIENTISTS WAS SABOTAGING HIS OWN RESEARCH.
SORRY I BLAMED YOUR FAMILY FOR SPRAYING MY MOM'S CROPS, IRENE. I GUESS WHEN BAD THINGS HAPPEN, IT'S EASY TO BLAME SOMEONE YOU DON'T REALLY KNOW.
DONT' SWEAT IT. WE HAVEN'T SPRAYED ANYTHING ON OUR CROPS SINCE WE BECAME AN ORGANIC FARM.
ORGANIC FARMERS DON'T USE CHEMICALS LIKE PESTICIDES OR FERTILIZERS TO GROW THEIR CROPS.
DOESN'T THAT MAKE IT HARDER TO KEEP THE PLANTS HEALTHY AND STOP BUGS FROM EATING THEM?
100% ORGANIC
ORGANIC JAM
ORGANIC PEPPER
ORGANIC CORN
WINDOVER FARM
ORGANIC EGGS
WE USE OTHER METHODS TO KEEP CROPS HEALTHY.
AND WE CREATE A SMALLER CARBON FOOTPRINT WHILE DOING IT. WHEN WE USE PESTICIDES, THAT IMPACT IS PERMANENT AND CAN TRAVEL WELL BEYOND THE FARM.

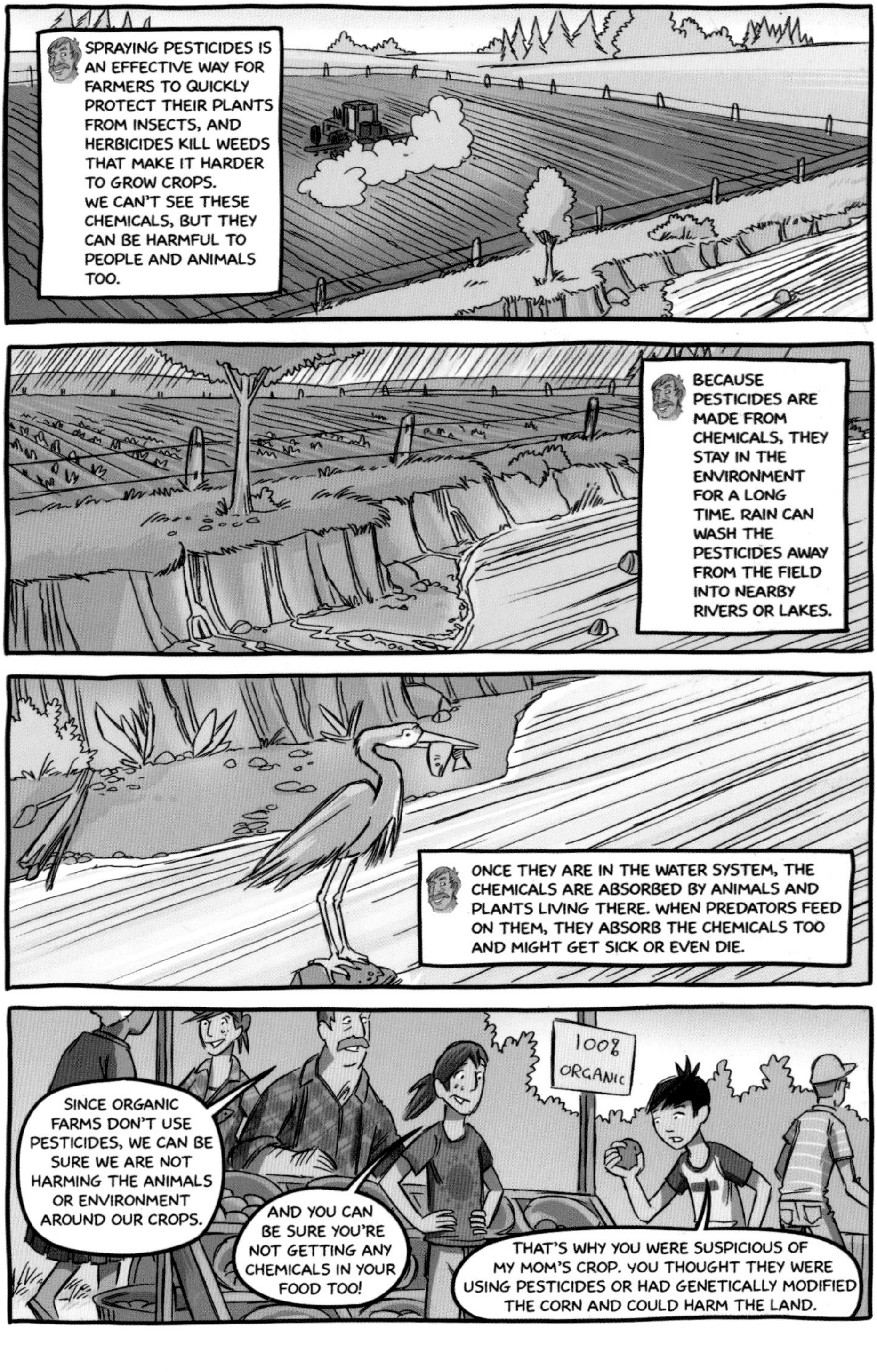
SPRAYING PESTICIDES IS AN EFFECTIVE WAY FOR FARMERS TO QUICKLY PROTECT THEIR PLANTS FROM INSECTS, AND HERBICIDES KILL WEEDS THAT MAKE IT HARDER TO GROW CROPS. WE CAN'T SEE THESE CHEMICALS, BUT THEY CAN BE HARMFUL TO PEOPLE AND ANIMALS TOO.
BECAUSE PESTICIDES ARE MADE FROM CHEMICALS, THEY STAY IN THE ENVIRONMENT FOR A LONG TIME. RAIN CAN WASH THE PESTICIDES AWAY FROM THE FIELD INTO NEARBY RIVERS OR LAKES.
ONCE THEY ARE IN THE WATER SYSTEM, THE CHEMICALS ARE ABSORBED BY ANIMALS AND PLANTS LIVING THERE. WHEN PREDATORS FEED ON THEM, THEY ABSORB THE CHEMICALS TOO AND MIGHT GET SICK OR EVEN DIE.
100% ORGANIC
SINCE ORGANIC FARMS DON'T USE PESTICIDES, WE CAN BE SURE WE ARE NOT HARMING THE ANIMALS OR ENVIRONMENT AROUND OUR CROPS.
AND YOU CAN BE SURE YOU'RE NOT GETTING ANY CHEMICALS IN YOUR FOOD TOO!
THAT'S WHY YOU WERE SUSPICIOUS OF MY MOM'S CROP. YOU THOUGHT THEY WERE USING PESTICIDES OR HAD GENETICALLY MODIFIED THE CORN AND COULD HARM THE LAND.

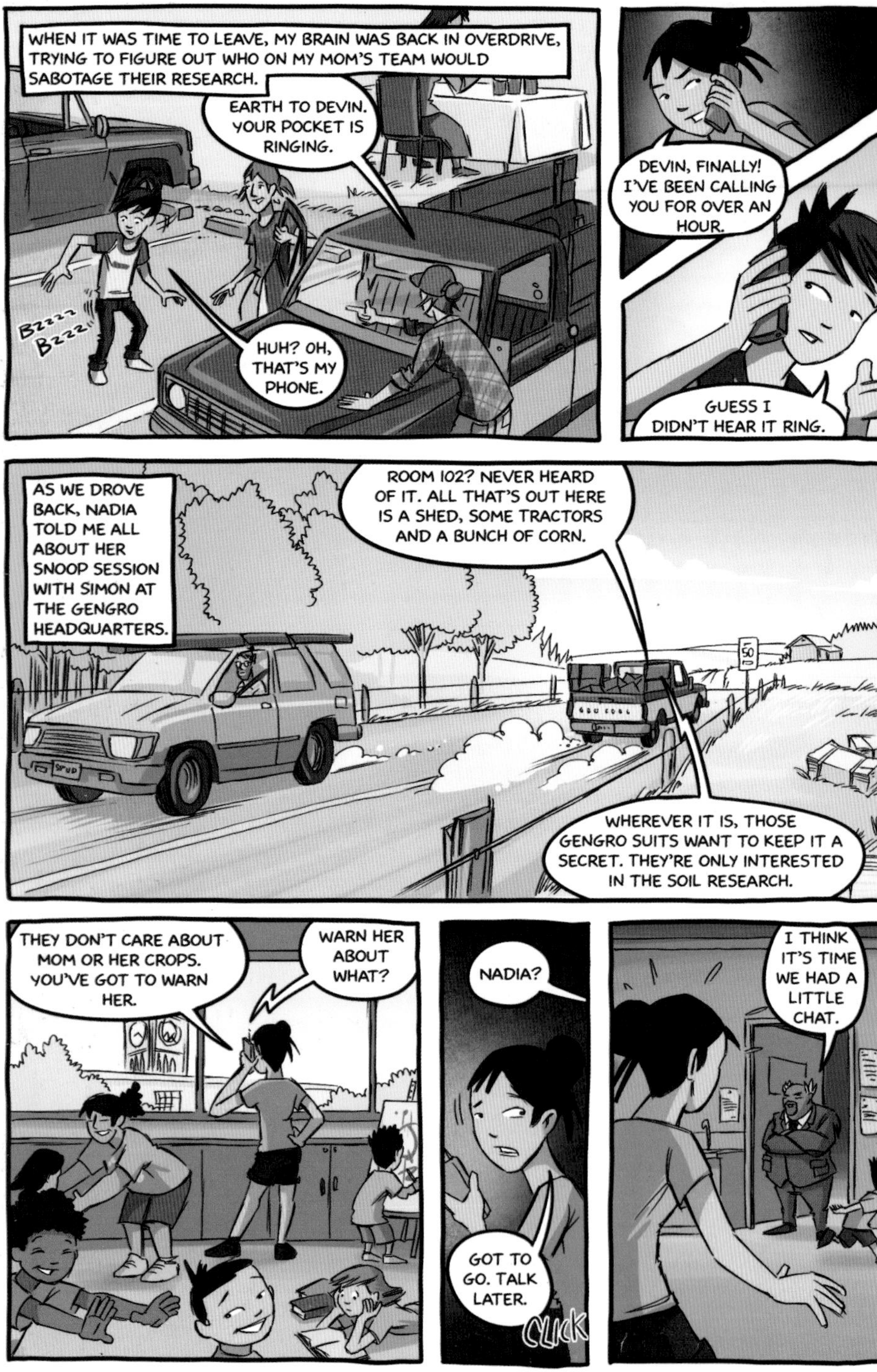
WHEN IT WAS TIME TO LEAVE, MY BRAIN WAS BACK IN OVERDRIVE, TRYING TO FIGURE OUT WHO ON MY MOM'S TEAM WOULD SABOTAGE THEIR RESEARCH.
EARTH TO DEVIN. YOUR POCKET IS RINGING.
BZZZZ BZZZ
HUH? OH, THAT'S MY PHONE.
DEVIN, FINALLY! I'VE BEEN CALLING YOU FOR OVER AN HOUR.
GUESS I DIDN'T HEAR IT RING.
AS WE DROVE BACK, NADIA TOLD ME ALL ABOUT HER SNOOP SESSION WITH SIMON AT THE GENGRO HEADQUARTERS.
ROOM 102? NEVER HEARD OF IT. ALL THAT'S OUT HERE IS A SHED, SOME TRACTORS AND A BUNCH OF CORN.
50
WHEREVER IT IS, THOSE GENGRO SUITS WANT TO KEEP IT A SECRET. THEY'RE ONLY INTERESTED IN THE SOIL RESEARCH.
THEY DON'T CARE ABOUT MOM OR HER CROPS. YOU'VE GOT TO WARN HER.
WARN HER ABOUT WHAT?
NADIA?
GOT TO GO. TALK LATER.
CLICK
I THINK IT'S TIME WE HAD A LITTLE CHAT.

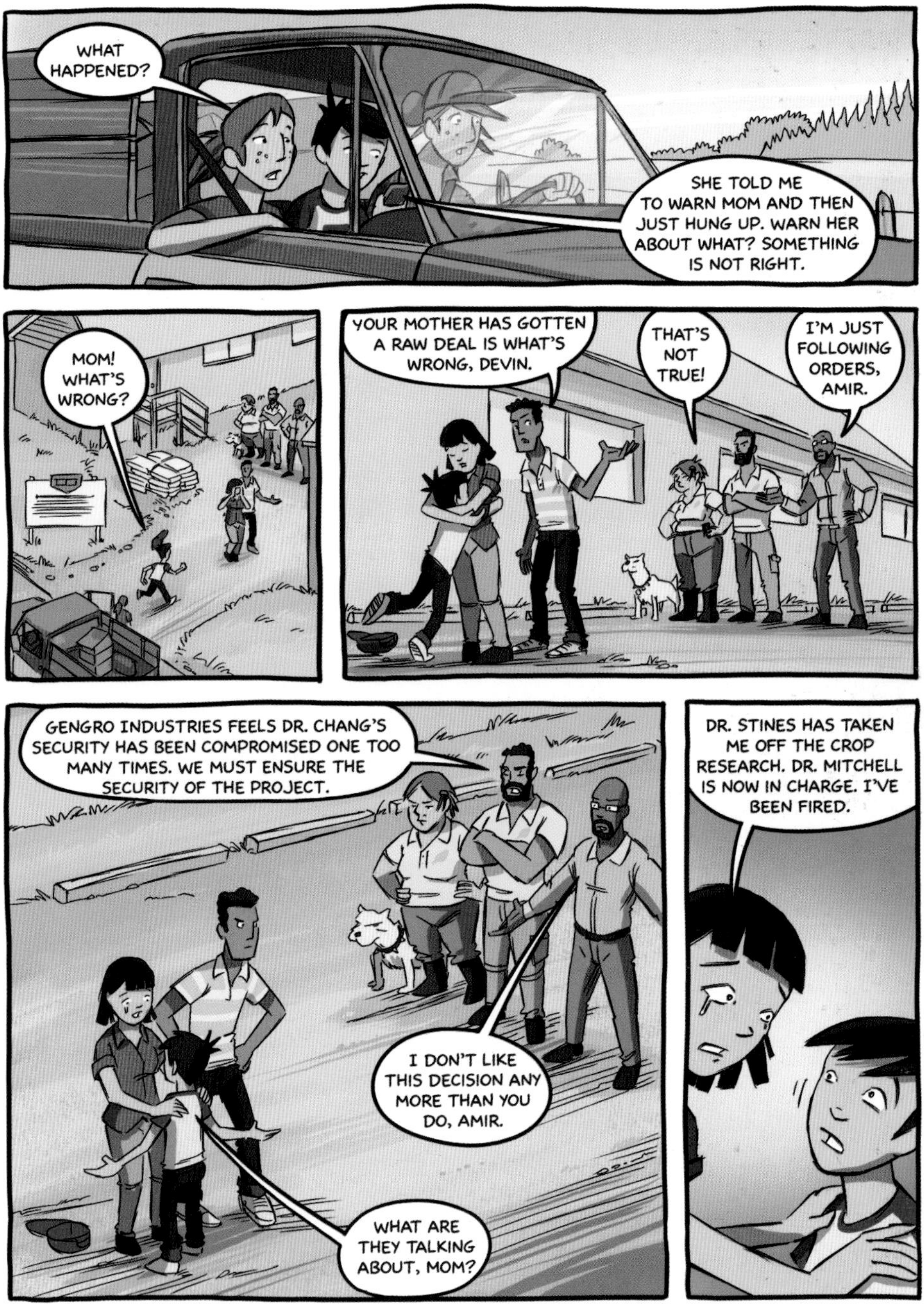
WHAT HAPPENED?
SHE TOLD ME TO WARN MOM AND THEN JUST HUNG UP. WARN HER ABOUT WHAT? SOMETHING IS NOT RIGHT.
MOM! WHAT'S WRONG?
YOUR MOTHER HAS GOTTEN A RAW DEAL IS WHAT'S WRONG, DEVIN.
THAT'S NOT TRUE!
I'M JUST FOLLOWING ORDERS, AMIR.
GENGRO INDUSTRIES FEELS DR. CHANG'S SECURITY HAS BEEN COMPROMISED ONE TOO MANY TIMES. WE MUST ENSURE THE SECURITY OF THE PROJECT.
I DON'T LIKE THIS DECISION ANY MORE THAN YOU DO, AMIR.
WHAT ARE THEY TALKING ABOUT, MOM?
DR. STINES HAS TAKEN ME OFF THE CROP RESEARCH. DR. MITCHELL IS NOW IN CHARGE. I'VE BEEN FIRED.

CHAPTER 5
SOIL SECRETS

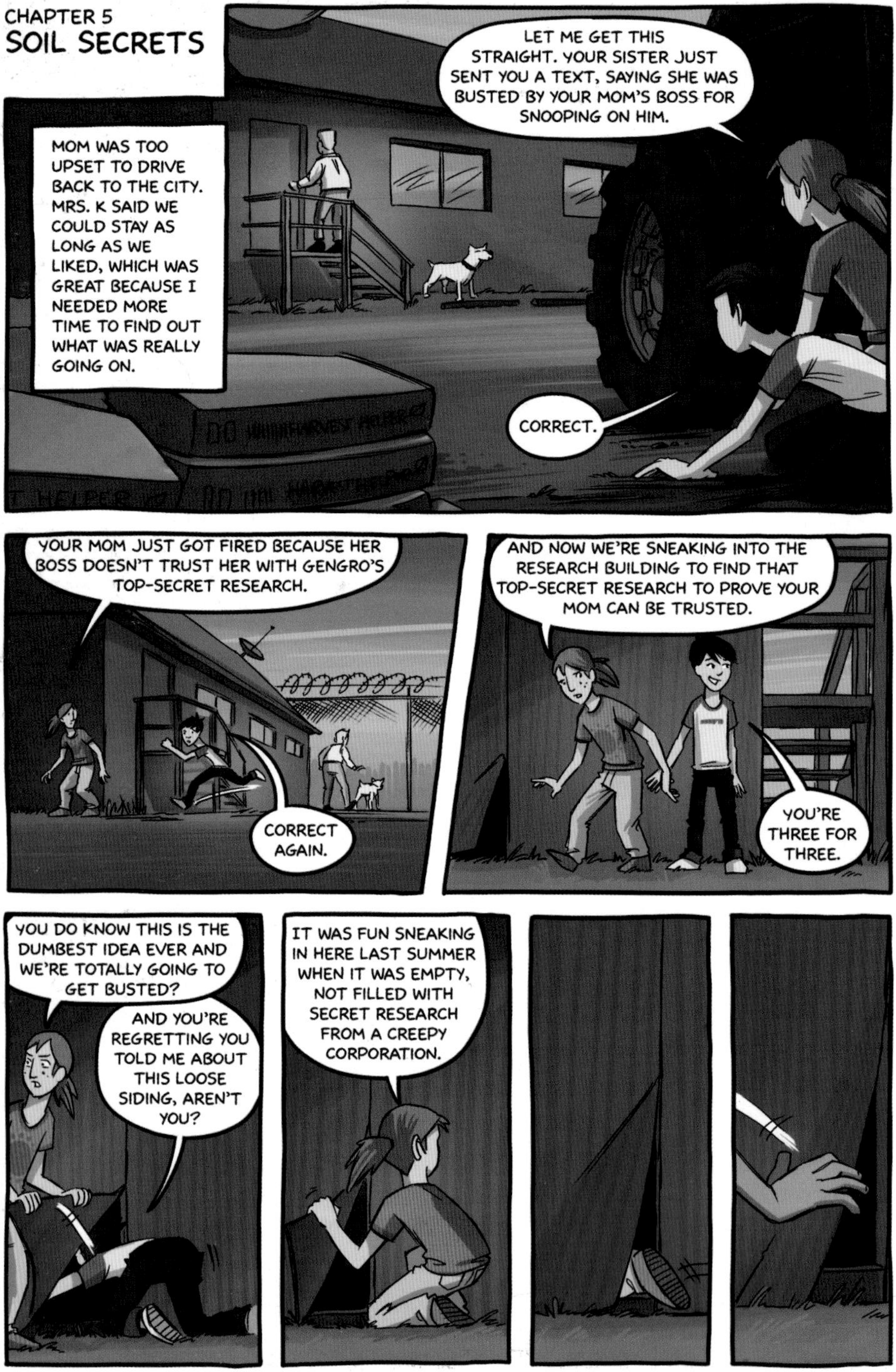
MOM WAS TOO UPSET TO DRIVE BACK TO THE CITY. MRS. K SAID WE COULD STAY AS LONG AS WE LIKED, WHICH WAS GREAT BECAUSE I NEEDED MORE TIME TO FIND OUT WHAT WAS REALLY GOING ON.
LET ME GET THIS STRAIGHT. YOUR SISTER JUST SENT YOU A TEXT, SAYING SHE WAS BUSTED BY YOUR MOM'S BOSS FOR SNOOPING ON HIM.
CORRECT.
YOUR MOM JUST GOT FIRED BECAUSE HER BOSS DOESN'T TRUST HER WITH GENGRO'S TOP-SECRET RESEARCH.
CORRECT AGAIN.
AND NOW WE'RE SNEAKING INTO THE RESEARCH BUILDING TO FIND THAT TOP-SECRET RESEARCH TO PROVE YOUR MOM CAN BE TRUSTED.
YOU'RE THREE FOR THREE.
YOU DO KNOW THIS IS THE DUMBEST IDEA EVER AND WE'RE TOTALLY GOING TO GET BUSTED?
AND YOU'RE REGRETTING YOU TOLD ME ABOUT THIS LOOSE SIDING, AREN'T YOU?
IT WAS FUN SNEAKING IN HERE LAST SUMMER WHEN IT WAS EMPTY, NOT FILLED WITH SECRET RESEARCH FROM A CREEPY CORPORATION.

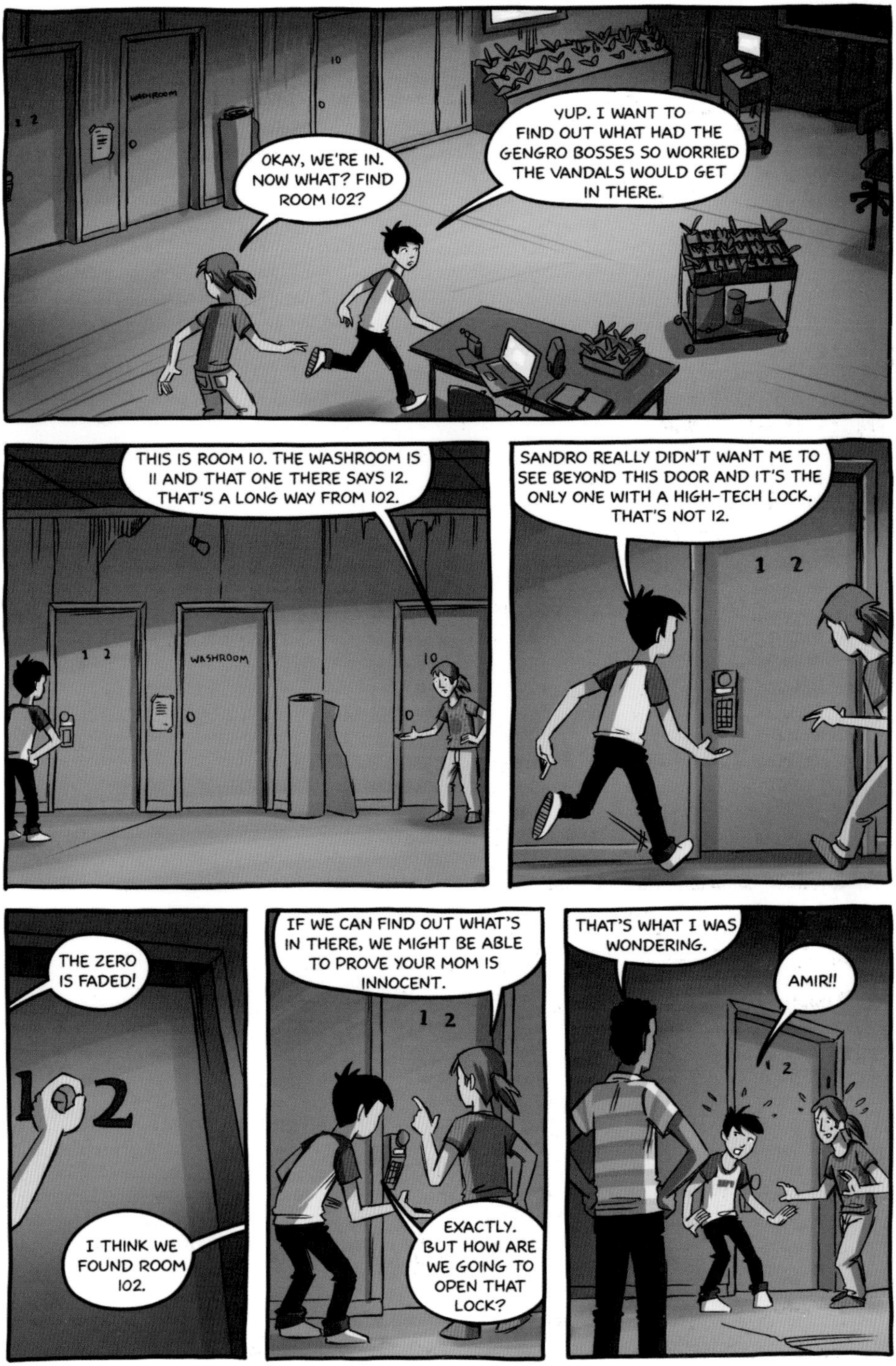

OKAY, WE'RE IN. NOW WHAT? FIND ROOM 102?
YUP. I WANT TO FIND OUT WHAT HAD THE GENGRO BOSSES SO WORRIED THE VANDALS WOULD GET IN THERE.
WASHROOM
10
THIS IS ROOM 10. THE WASHROOM IS 11 AND THAT ONE THERE SAYS 12. THAT'S A LONG WAY FROM 102.
1 2
WASHROOM
10
SANDRO REALLY DIDN'T WANT ME TO SEE BEYOND THIS DOOR AND IT'S THE ONLY ONE WITH A HIGH-TECH LOCK. THAT'S NOT 12.
1 2
THE ZERO IS FADED!
102
I THINK WE FOUND ROOM 102.
IF WE CAN FIND OUT WHAT'S IN THERE, WE MIGHT BE ABLE TO PROVE YOUR MOM IS INNOCENT.
1 2
EXACTLY. BUT HOW ARE WE GOING TO OPEN THAT LOCK?
THAT'S WHAT I WAS WONDERING.
AMIR!!

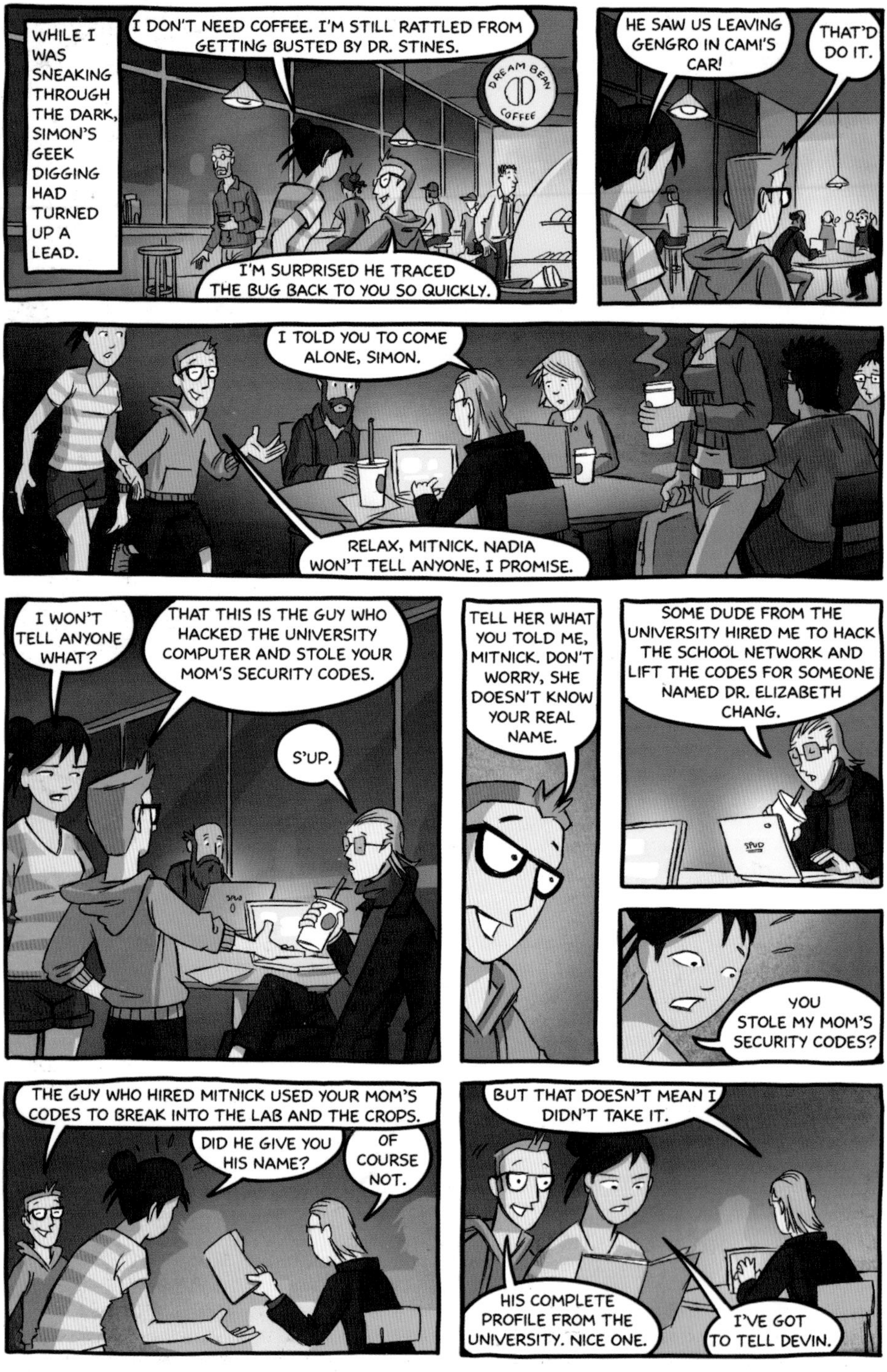
WHILE I WAS SNEAKING THROUGH THE DARK, SIMON'S GEEK DIGGING HAD TURNED UP A LEAD.
I DON'T NEED COFFEE. I'M STILL RATTLED FROM GETTING BUSTED BY DR. STINES.
DREAM BEAN COFFEE
I'M SURPRISED HE TRACED THE BUG BACK TO YOU SO QUICKLY.
HE SAW US LEAVING GENGRO IN CAMI'S CAR!
THAT'D DO IT.
I TOLD YOU TO COME ALONE, SIMON.
RELAX, MITNICK. NADIA WON'T TELL ANYONE, I PROMISE.
I WON'T TELL ANYONE WHAT?
THAT THIS IS THE GUY WHO HACKED THE UNIVERSITY COMPUTER AND STOLE YOUR MOM'S SECURITY CODES.
S'UP.
TELL HER WHAT YOU TOLD ME, MITNICK. DON'T WORRY, SHE DOESN'T KNOW YOUR REAL NAME.
SOME DUDE FROM THE UNIVERSITY HIRED ME TO HACK THE SCHOOL NETWORK AND LIFT THE CODES FOR SOMEONE NAMED DR. ELIZABETH CHANG.
SPUD
YOU STOLE MY MOM'S SECURITY CODES?
THE GUY WHO HIRED MITNICK USED YOUR MOM'S CODES TO BREAK INTO THE LAB AND THE CROPS.
DID HE GIVE YOU HIS NAME?
OF COURSE NOT.
BUT THAT DOESN'T MEAN I DIDN'T TAKE IT.
HIS COMPLETE PROFILE FROM THE UNIVERSITY. NICE ONE.
I'VE GOT TO TELL DEVIN.

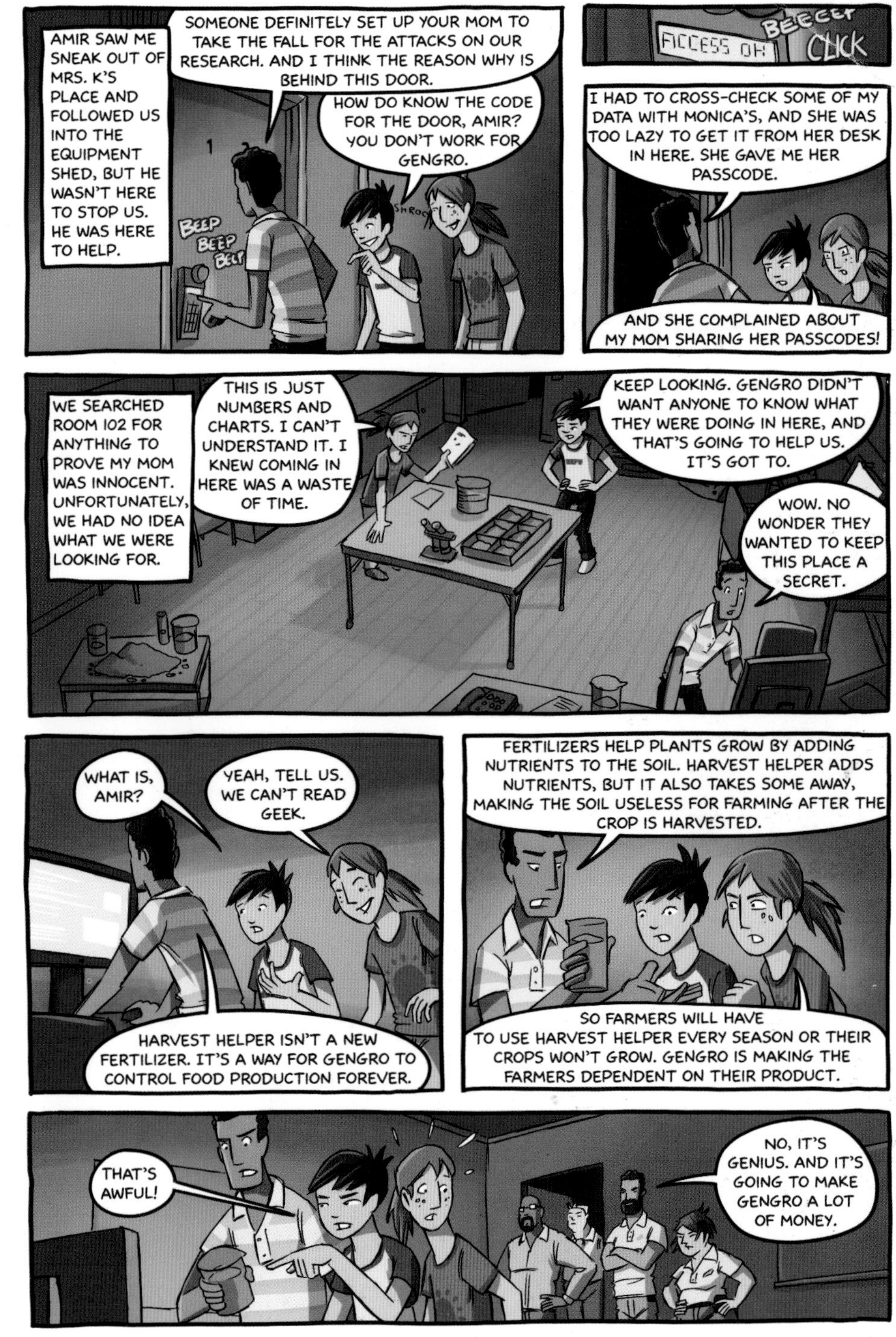
AMIR SAW ME SNEAK OUT OF MRS. K'S PLACE AND FOLLOWED US INTO THE EQUIPMENT SHED, BUT HE WASN'T HERE TO STOP US. HE WAS HERE TO HELP.
SOMEONE DEFINITELY SET UP YOUR MOM TO TAKE THE FALL FOR THE ATTACKS ON OUR RESEARCH. AND I THINK THE REASON WHY IS BEHIND THIS DOOR.
HOW DO KNOW THE CODE FOR THE DOOR, AMIR? YOU DON'T WORK FOR GENGRO.
BEEP
BEEP
ACCESS OK
CLICK
I HAD TO CROSS-CHECK SOME OF MY DATA WITH MONICA'S, AND SHE WAS TOO LAZY TO GET IT FROM HER DESK IN HERE. SHE GAVE ME HER PASSCODE.
AND SHE COMPLAINED ABOUT MY MOM SHARING HER PASSCODES!
WE SEARCHED ROOM 102 FOR ANYTHING TO PROVE MY MOM WAS INNOCENT. UNFORTUNATELY, WE HAD NO IDEA WHAT WE WERE LOOKING FOR.
THIS IS JUST NUMBERS AND CHARTS. I CAN'T UNDERSTAND IT. I KNEW COMING IN HERE WAS A WASTE OF TIME.
KEEP LOOKING. GENGRO DIDN'T WANT ANYONE TO KNOW WHAT THEY WERE DOING IN HERE, AND THAT'S GOING TO HELP US. IT'S GOT TO.
WOW. NO WONDER THEY WANTED TO KEEP THIS PLACE A SECRET.
WHAT IS, AMIR?
YEAH, TELL US. WE CAN'T READ GEEK.
HARVEST HELPER ISN'T A NEW FERTILIZER. IT'S A WAY FOR GENGRO TO CONTROL FOOD PRODUCTION FOREVER.
FERTILIZERS HELP PLANTS GROW BY ADDING NUTRIENTS TO THE SOIL. HARVEST HELPER ADDS NUTRIENTS, BUT IT ALSO TAKES SOME AWAY, MAKING THE SOIL USELESS FOR FARMING AFTER THE CROP IS HARVESTED.
SO FARMERS WILL HAVE TO USE HARVEST HELPER EVERY SEASON OR THEIR CROPS WON'T GROW. GENGRO IS MAKING THE FARMERS DEPENDENT ON THEIR PRODUCT.
THAT'S AWFUL!
NO, IT'S GENIUS. AND IT'S GOING TO MAKE GENGRO A LOT OF MONEY.

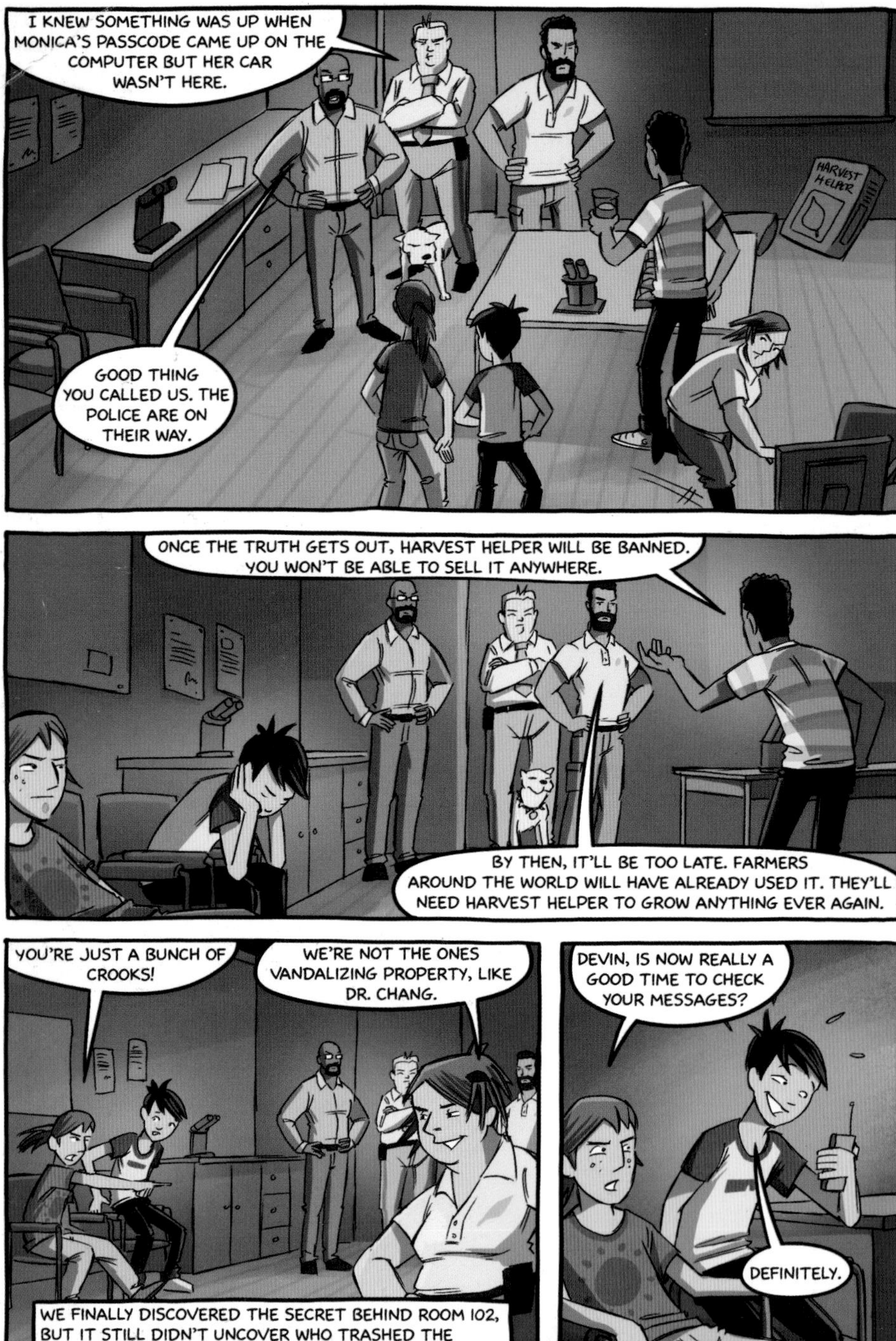
I KNEW SOMETHING WAS UP WHEN MONICA'S PASSCODE CAME UP ON THE COMPUTER BUT HER CAR WASN'T HERE.
GOOD THING YOU CALLED US. THE POLICE ARE ON THEIR WAY.
HARVEST HELPER
ONCE THE TRUTH GETS OUT, HARVEST HELPER WILL BE BANNED. YOU WON'T BE ABLE TO SELL IT ANYWHERE.
BY THEN, IT'LL BE TOO LATE. FARMERS AROUND THE WORLD WILL HAVE ALREADY USED IT. THEY'LL NEED HARVEST HELPER TO GROW ANYTHING EVER AGAIN.
YOU'RE JUST A BUNCH OF CROOKS!
WE'RE NOT THE ONES VANDALIZING PROPERTY, LIKE DR. CHANG.
WE FINALLY DISCOVERED THE SECRET BEHIND ROOM 102, BUT IT STILL DIDN'T UNCOVER WHO TRASHED THE CROPS. THEN SUDDENLY, MY PANTS STARTED BUZZING.
DEVIN, IS NOW REALLY A GOOD TIME TO CHECK YOUR MESSAGES?
DEFINITELY.

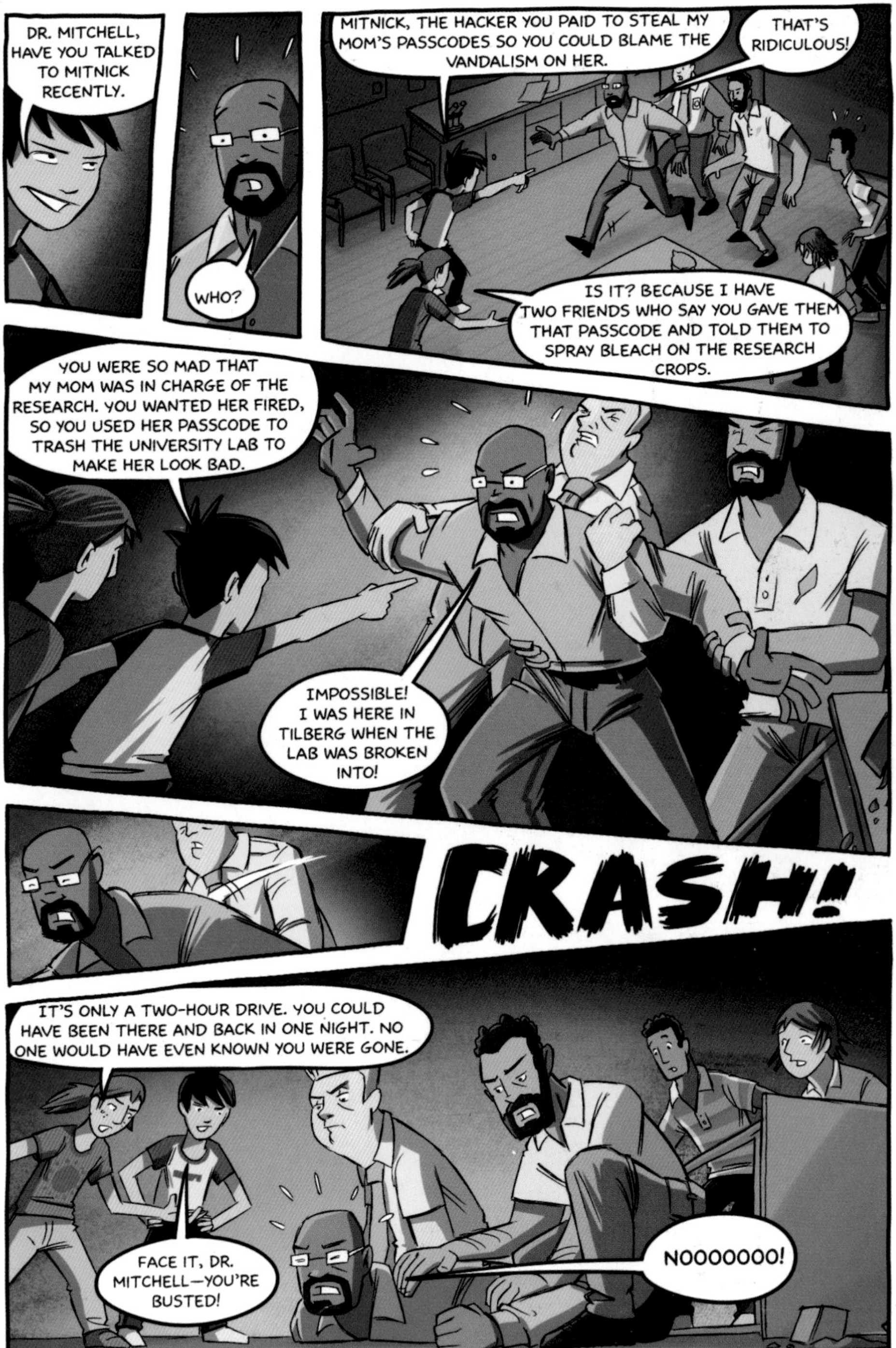
DR. MITCHELL, HAVE YOU TALKED TO MITNICK RECENTLY.
WHO?
MITNICK, THE HACKER YOU PAID TO STEAL MY MOM'S PASSCODES SO YOU COULD BLAME THE VANDALISM ON HER.
THAT'S RIDICULOUS!
IS IT? BECAUSE I HAVE TWO FRIENDS WHO SAY YOU GAVE THEM THAT PASSCODE AND TOLD THEM TO SPRAY BLEACH ON THE RESEARCH CROPS.
YOU WERE SO MAD THAT MY MOM WAS IN CHARGE OF THE RESEARCH. YOU WANTED HER FIRED, SO YOU USED HER PASSCODE TO TRASH THE UNIVERSITY LAB TO MAKE HER LOOK BAD.
IMPOSSIBLE! I WAS HERE IN TILBERG WHEN THE LAB WAS BROKEN INTO!
CRASH!
IT'S ONLY A TWO-HOUR DRIVE. YOU COULD HAVE BEEN THERE AND BACK IN ONE NIGHT. NO ONE WOULD HAVE EVEN KNOWN YOU WERE GONE.
FACE IT, DR. MITCHELL—YOU'RE BUSTED!
NOOOOOOO!

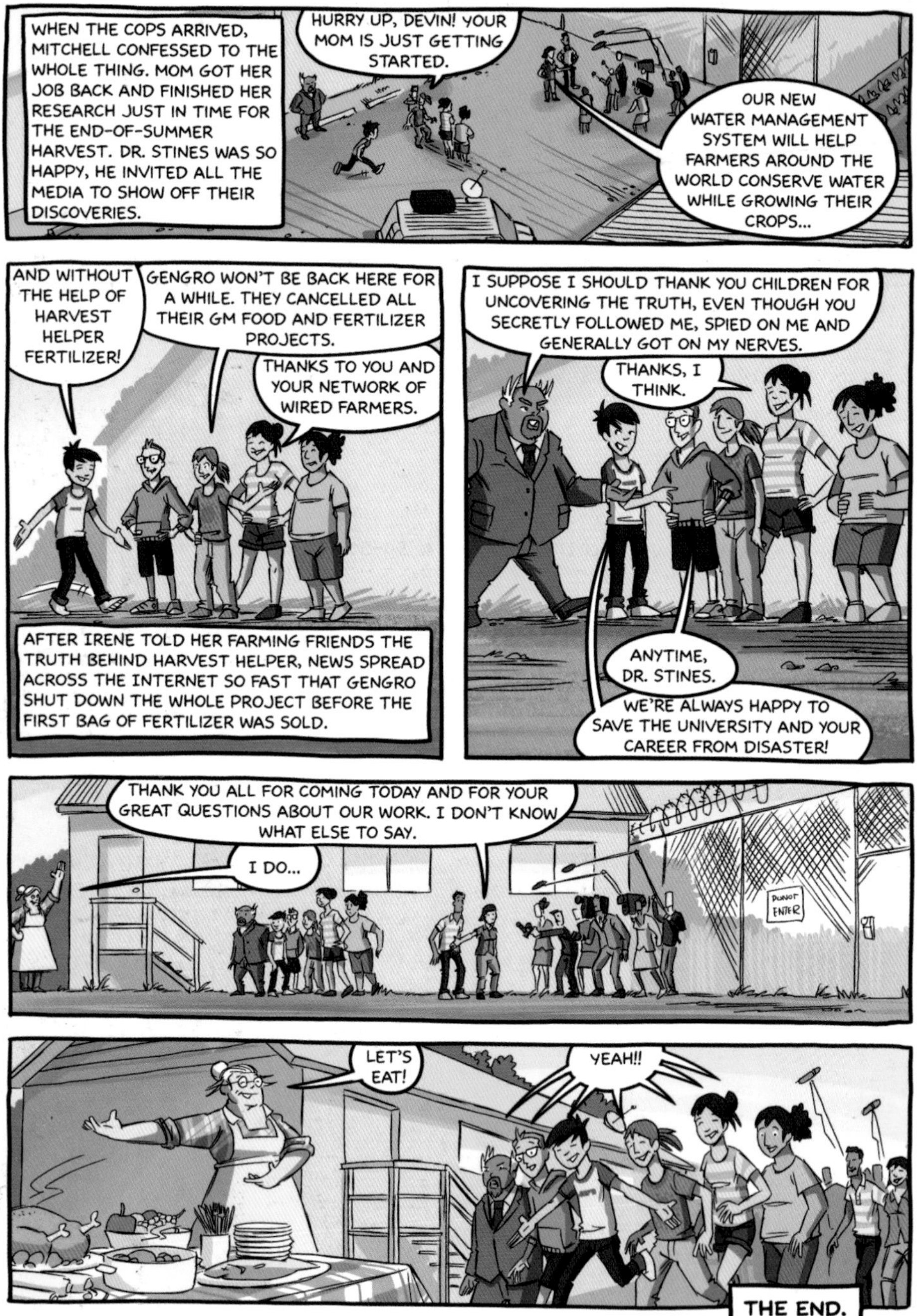
WHEN THE COPS ARRIVED, MITCHELL CONFESSED TO THE WHOLE THING. MOM GOT HER JOB BACK AND FINISHED HER RESEARCH JUST IN TIME FOR THE END-OF-SUMMER HARVEST. DR. STINES WAS SO HAPPY, HE INVITED ALL THE MEDIA TO SHOW OFF THEIR DISCOVERIES.
HURRY UP, DEVIN! YOUR MOM IS JUST GETTING STARTED.
OUR NEW WATER MANAGEMENT SYSTEM WILL HELP FARMERS AROUND THE WORLD CONSERVE WATER WHILE GROWING THEIR CROPS...
AND WITHOUT THE HELP OF HARVEST HELPER FERTILIZER!
GENGRO WON'T BE BACK HERE FOR A WHILE. THEY CANCELLED ALL THEIR GM FOOD AND FERTILIZER PROJECTS.
THANKS TO YOU AND YOUR NETWORK OF WIRED FARMERS.
AFTER IRENE TOLD HER FARMING FRIENDS THE TRUTH BEHIND HARVEST HELPER, NEWS SPREAD ACROSS THE INTERNET SO FAST THAT GENGRO SHUT DOWN THE WHOLE PROJECT BEFORE THE FIRST BAG OF FERTILIZER WAS SOLD.
I SUPPOSE I SHOULD THANK YOU CHILDREN FOR UNCOVERING THE TRUTH, EVEN THOUGH YOU SECRETLY FOLLOWED ME, SPIED ON ME AND GENERALLY GOT ON MY NERVES.
THANKS, I THINK.
ANYTIME, DR. STINES.
WE'RE ALWAYS HAPPY TO SAVE THE UNIVERSITY AND YOUR CAREER FROM DISASTER!
THANK YOU ALL FOR COMING TODAY AND FOR YOUR GREAT QUESTIONS ABOUT OUR WORK. I DON'T KNOW WHAT ELSE TO SAY.
I DO...
DO NOT ENTER
LET'S EAT!
YEAH!!
THE END.

Grab these other Graphic Guide Adventures...

WILD RIDE
A GRAPHIC GUIDE ADVENTURE
LIAM O'DONNELL
MIKE DEAS

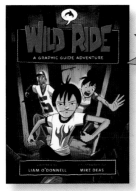

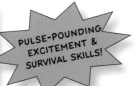

PULSE-POUNDING EXCITEMENT & SURVIVAL SKILLS!

AFTER THEIR PLANE GOES DOWN IN RUGGED WILDERNESS, DEVIN, NADIA AND MARCUS STRUGGLE TO SURVIVE. ADVENTURE, DANGER AND SURVIVAL SKILLS (AND BEARS. OH MY!).

978-1-55143-756-9

EXCITEMENT, ACTION & SOME RADICAL SKATING TIPS!

RAMP RATS
A GRAPHIC GUIDE ADVENTURE
WRITTEN BY
LIAM O'DONNELL
ILLUSTRATED BY
MIKE DEAS

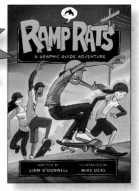

BETWEEN LEARNING HOW TO OLLIE AND DO A 50-50 GRIND, BOUNCE AND HIS FRIENDS HAVE TO AVOID THE SKATE-PARK GOONS AND TAKE ON A GANG OF OUTLAW BIKERS. A JUNIOR LIBRARY GUILD SELECTION.

978-1-55143-880-1

SOCCER SABOTAGE
A GRAPHIC GUIDE ADVENTURE
WRITTEN BY
LIAM O'DONNELL
ILLUSTRATED BY
MIKE DEAS

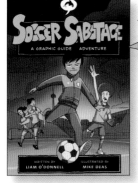

ACTION, ADVENTURE AND SOME SPOT-ON SOCCER INSTRUCTION!

WITH SUSPICIOUS ACCIDENTS AND MOUNTING THREATS AGAINST THE TEAM, IT'S UP TO DEVIN AND HIS SISTER NADIA TO PULL THE TEAM TOGETHER AND TAKE A RUN AT THE CHAMPIONSHIP.

978-1-55143-884-9

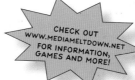

CHECK OUT WWW.MEDIAMELTDOWN.NET FOR INFORMATION, GAMES AND MORE!

MEDIA MELTDOWN
A GRAPHIC GUIDE ADVENTURE
WRITTEN BY
LIAM O'DONNELL
ILLUSTRATED BY
MIKE DEAS

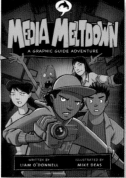

WHEN A DEVELOPER TRIES TO FORCE THE SALE OF A LOCAL FARM, PEMA, BOUNCE AND JAGROOP DECIDE TO EXPOSE HIM THROUGH THE MEDIA. SOME FRIGHTENING LESSONS ABOUT MEDIA CONSOLIDATION AND THE POWER OF MONEY OVER TRUTH.

978-1-55469-065-7

And coming in Fall 2010—Power Play!

ABOUT THE AUTHOR

FROM CHAPTER BOOKS TO COMIC STRIPS, LIAM O'DONNELL WRITES FICTION AND NONFICTION FOR YOUNG READERS. HE IS THE AUTHOR OF THE AWARD-WINNING SERIES "MAX FINDER MYSTERY." LIAM LIVES IN TORONTO, ONTARIO.

ABOUT THE ILLUSTRATOR

MIKE DEAS IS A TALENTED ILLUSTRATOR IN A NUMBER OF DIFFERENT GENRES. HE GRADUATED FROM CAPILANO COLLEGE'S COMMERCIAL ANIMATION PROGRAM AND HAS WORKED AS A GAME DEVELOPER. MIKE LIVES IN VICTORIA, BRITISH COLUMBIA.